"Did they look all right to you?"

He leaned back in the saddle at the odd question. "I suppose," he said. When he started to speak again, the words died in his throat as the woman approached and he got his first good look at her.

Oval face, slender nose, bow-shaped lips. And those eyes—large, dark and luminous, fringed by impossibly long lashes.

"Isabel," he whispered hoarsely.

Her brown eyes grew wide as s███ ███████ ███. "Wyatt," she choked out. Sh█ ████ ████ ███ couldn't believe what ██ ███ █████.

He understood the ████ ██████ ████████ ███ through him, tighter █████ ███ ███████ ███ ███ it hard to breathe. It had bee█ ██ █████ ███ he'd last seen her. Ten years sin███ ████ ██ade love in the bed of his pickup unde███ ██ket of stars. Ten years since she'd stolen his heart, then walked away without a backward glance.

There was so much he wanted to say, to ask. So much he wanted to know. A decade's worth of questions tumbled in his brain, each jockeying for prominence. But as he opened his mouth, only two words slipped out.

"You're back."

* * *

Dear Reader,

Welcome back to Big Bend, Texas! I enjoy writing these books because I love to tell stories set in my home state. Big Bend National Park is a truly special place, and I hope that my books do it justice.

This was a fun book to write. I loved getting to know Wyatt and Isabel, and watching them overcome the hurts from their shared past to face the future together. They're up against some steep odds, both personally and professionally. I hope you enjoy reading about their attempts to discover who is threatening the Cruz family ranch. With so many suspects, will they ever know for sure?

Happy reading!

Lara

THE RANGER'S
REUNION THREAT

Lara Lacombe

HARLEQUIN®
ROMANTIC
SUSPENSE™

Recycling programs
for this product may
not exist in your area.

ISBN-13: 978-1-335-62646-2

The Ranger's Reunion Threat

Copyright © 2020 by Lara Kingeter

This edition published by arrangement with Harlequin Books S.A.

For questions and comments about the quality of this book, please contact us at CustomerService@Harlequin.com.

Harlequin Enterprises ULC
22 Adelaide St. West, 40th Floor
Toronto, Ontario M5H 4E3, Canada
www.Harlequin.com

Printed in U.S.A.

Lara Lacombe earned a PhD in microbiology and immunology and worked in several labs across the country before moving into the classroom. Her day job as a college science professor gives her time to pursue her other love—writing fast-paced romantic suspense with smart, nerdy heroines and dangerously attractive heroes. She loves to hear from readers! Find her on the web or contact her at laralacombewriter@gmail.com.

Books by Lara Lacombe

Harlequin Romantic Suspense

Visit the Author Profile page at Harlequin.com for more titles.

This one is for EKRS, best friend extraordinaire

Chapter 1

Her horse scented the blood before she did.

It was a gorgeous spring day, the sun high in the sky and the air warm and smelling of grass. Isabel Cruz was riding along the fence line, out on a routine patrol. Her family's cattle ranch shared a border with Big Bend National Park, and it was important to regularly check the fences to ensure none of their cattle escaped into the park. With calving season about to start, this was the kind of routine chore that would move to the bottom of the list once things got really busy. As the ranch's resident veterinarian, she relished this mundane job, knowing her free time would soon disappear. When a calving went well, there wasn't much for her to do. But when things went wrong, she was up to her armpits in work.

Literally.

One minute, she was enjoying the sun on her back and the steady, loping gait of the horse under her. Then, without warning, her mount shied, rearing back and jerking violently to the left.

Isabel's legs tightened on the saddle as she shifted her weight to keep her seat. "Whoa, Miel," she said, keeping her voice calm to avoid further spooking the animal. "It's all right."

The mare was clearly distressed, her nostrils flaring and her eyes wide as she danced in place, inching backward as much as she was able. Isabel eased her grip on the reins, allowing the animal to move away from whatever it was that had bothered her.

Miel settled down after traveling a few feet. Knowing better than to urge her forward again, Isabel dismounted and looped the reins around one of the support posts of the fence. Then she set off on foot, heading back for the troubling spot.

She saw the fence first. A section of the barbed wire barrier was missing, creating a wide gap. Isabel swore softly as she studied the situation. This wasn't the kind of breakdown caused by exposure to wind and weather; someone had cut through the panel, making no effort to hide their sabotage.

Probably hikers, she thought sourly. Even though there were No Trespassing signs posted at regular intervals along the fence that marked the border with the park, it wasn't uncommon for backpackers to steal onto the ranch for a quick drink and dip in one of the many watering holes on the property. This particular spot was frequently tampered with as one such small pond was clearly visible from the nearby trail. Most people took their chances scaling the barbed wire, but this culprit had removed a three-foot stretch to gain entrance to the ranch property. The gap was wide enough for cattle to easily pass into the park, which created another set of problems…

Isabel reached for her walkie-talkie. She had a few supplies in her saddlebags—enough to make a quick repair. But the whole panel needed to be replaced, something that required more material than she had on hand. And they'd need to find out if any animals had crossed into Big Bend. If the park rangers found Cruz cattle inside the park, they'd round them up and sell them at auction. The ranch would likely be fined, as well. It was an outcome the ranch could ill afford right now.

Just as she brought the device to her lips, the wind changed direction. The breeze fluttered over her, carrying the unmistakable stench of death. *Ah*, she thought. *So that's the problem.*

Behind her, Miel let out a distressed whinny. "You're okay, my sweet," Isabel called out. The mare was a good-natured animal, but she was still learning how to be a cattle horse and adjusting to all the sights, sounds and smells that that entailed. Most of the working horses on the ranch were unfazed by death, but a few still reacted strongly to the scent of blood. It seemed Miel was one of them.

Isabel walked through the grass and low scrub, searching for the source of the stench. The herd lost a cow or two every season, thanks to the efforts of local predators like mountain lions. The heavily pregnant cows were brought closer to the barn so they could be watched for signs of impending labor, but it was possible one of the other animals had taken lame and been unable to outrun a big cat.

A heavy buzzing filled the air, growing louder as she walked. *Getting closer*, she thought grimly. Flies and other insects wasted no time when there was a meal to be had. All part of the circle of life…

At the edge of a small declivity, she saw them. Her heart sank as she counted; three cows down. That in itself was unusual—a mountain lion could take down one cow on a good day, but three? Unheard of.

Isabel frowned as she approached the carcasses. All three cows lay a few steps away from each other, but aside from a couple of spots here and there where the buzzards had started in, there were no obvious injuries to be seen.

Disease? As a large animal veterinarian, she'd had experience with some of the many pathogens that could sicken and kill cattle. The ranch hands were always on the lookout for signs of illness, and any sick cow was quickly separated from the herd and evaluated.

She walked slowly toward the heads of the animals, running her gaze over their bodies in search of any telltale symptoms. Nothing jumped out, but then again, there were several diseases that could only be identified after performing a necropsy and taking tissue samples.

"Damn," she muttered. It looked like she was going to have a busy night.

She lifted the walkie-talkie to her lips. "Diego, come in."

There was a burst of static across the line. "What's up, sis?"

"I've got three head of cattle down out here along the east fence."

"Sorry, you're breaking up. I thought I heard you say three."

"I did," she confirmed grimly.

"What the hell is going on out there?" Her brother's surprise matched her own.

"I won't know until I get them home and open them up. Send the flatbed, please." She told him about the damaged fence, as well.

He cursed. "Ruben and I will round up everything and be there shortly. Let me know if anything changes."

"Will do. Over and out."

Isabel clipped the walkie-talkie back onto her belt and stared at the animals at her feet. She walked over to the head of one and squatted, waving away the flies so she could get a better look.

A thin track of dried blood ran from the cow's nose, but she saw no lesions or any other marks that might indicate what had caused these animals to die. Part of her wanted to get closer, but she knew that without the proper safety precautions, she should leave things alone. If these cows had been infected with something, the last thing she needed was to catch it, as well.

"What happened to you?" she said softly, studying the closest animal. "And how can I stop it from happening to the others?"

Park ranger Wyatt Spalding rose in the saddle and squinted into the distance. Were those...cows?

He nudged his mount forward. As he got closer, he realized his first impression had been correct. Five cows stood in the small valley, chomping placidly on clumps of grass. They eyed him curiously as he approached, but didn't seem bothered by his presence.

"Uh, hi, ladies," he said, pushing up the brim of his hat. "You look lost."

The cow closest to him flicked her tail at that, but otherwise didn't respond. Wyatt guided his horse to her left side, wanting to get a look at the flanks of the animals.

It wasn't unusual to see rogue livestock here. There were a few working outfits that shared a border with the park and while fences separated ranch from park land, every once in a while, a determined cow slipped through. Animals often crossed the shallow stretches of the Rio Grande in search of greener pastures, as well.

These cows sported a backward *C* snugged up against the letter *R*. Wyatt recognized the brand immediately. It was the marking for Cruz Ranch, one of the oldest family establishments in the area.

"Well, hell," he muttered to himself. Protocol stated he needed to call this in so that the response team could bring out trailers and haul the animals away. Livestock that trespassed on park land were usually rounded up, held in quarantine and then auctioned off to the highest bidder.

The problem was, he was friends with Diego Cruz, grandson and heir to the ranch owner, Jose Cruz. The family usually ran a tight ship when it came to keeping their animals off of park land. In fact, Wyatt could count on one hand the number of times Cruz cattle had been found in Big Bend, and he'd still have a few fingers left over. The fact he'd found five rogue animals meant something was wrong.

Wyatt was torn between the desire to help an old friend and the responsibility to follow the rules. He hated to pile trouble onto Diego, but it was his job to protect the park. Cows weren't at the top of most people's list of dangerous animals, but they were steady grazers who could clear a patch of grass in a matter of hours. He had to get these animals out of here, the sooner the better.

Maybe he could just "encourage" the animals to

head home and then talk to Diego about the situation. One free pass wasn't the end of the world, and he knew a lot of the nearby ranches were struggling financially. The cattle market wasn't what it used to be and this was an unforgiving land, especially in the summer. Most ranchers had to bring in food and water for their herds, often at exorbitant costs. The loss of these cows and the accompanying fine would just add to Diego's difficulties.

He took off his hat and ran a hand through his hair. "You look like you're enjoying yourself, but it's time to head on home," he said to the nearest cow.

She continued to ignore him as he donned his hat once more. But when he began to dismount, intending on giving his horse, Ajax, a break, the cow let out a startled bellow.

Apparently this was a signal. The cattle began to move, ears back, tails swishing as they walked in the direction of the ranch.

"Hey, wait!" Wyatt found himself in the awkward position of one foot in the stirrup, one on the ground. He boosted himself back up into the saddle, earning a soft grunt from Ajax. "I know, I know," he said to his horse. "But it's not my fault. Let's go."

He set off after the cattle, hoping they'd stay together. Ajax was no cattle horse. And while Wyatt had spent a summer in high school punching cows, he'd never made a good cowboy.

Fortunately for him, the animals stayed in a group as they trudged the mile or so back to the ranch. Like large, brown homing pigeons, the animals headed for a break in the wire fence, slipping through in a single-file line. Wyatt stopped and watched them walk toward the small pond about fifty yards away; apparently illegal grazing was thirsty work.

Ajax nickered a welcome. Wyatt glanced to the right and noticed a pretty bay mare standing by a clump of bushes. She was saddled, but there was no rider to be seen.

Wyatt frowned. That seemed odd.

"Hello?" he called loudly. Where was the rider? Had he come out to repair the fence and gotten hurt somehow? The mare seemed a little anxious, but perhaps that was simply due to their presence.

A movement to his left caught his eye. Wyatt turned and saw a head pop up out of the grass. Because of a small declivity in the land a few yards away, he could see some indeterminate dark shapes but nothing more.

"Hello." The voice that reached his ears was decidedly feminine, and Wyatt felt a rush of embarrassment as he realized he must have interrupted this lady's bathroom break.

"Uh, I'm sorry to bother you. It's just that five of your cattle were grazing in the park." He nodded to the animals in question, now all drinking from the pond nearby. "They must have slipped through the fence."

"Did they look all right to you?"

He leaned back in the saddle at the odd question.

"I suppose," he said. As he started to speak again, the words died in his throat when the woman approached and he got his first good look at her.

Oval face, slender nose, bow-shaped lips. And those eyes—large, dark and luminous, fringed by impossibly long lashes.

"Isabel," he whispered hoarsely.

Her brown eyes grew wide as she stared up at him. "Wyatt," she choked out. She blinked hard, as if she couldn't believe what she was seeing.

He understood the feeling. Emotions rushed through him, tightening his chest and making it hard to breathe. It had been ten years since he'd last seen her. Ten years since they'd made love in the bed of his pickup under a blanket of stars. Ten years since she'd stolen his heart then walked away without a backward glance.

There was so much he wanted to say, to ask. So much he wanted to know. A decade's worth of questions tumbled in his brain, each jockeying for prominence. But as he opened his mouth, only two words slipped out.

"You're back."

Chapter 2

I'm not ready for this.

As she stared up at Wyatt, looking larger than life on the back of his big chestnut horse, Isabel's stomach churned. The shadow cast over his face from the brim of his hat did nothing to dim the brightness of his blue eyes. They were just as beautiful as she'd remembered, the color of a cloudless summer sky.

Her gaze tracked over his face, noting the subtle changes wrought by time. His nose was still a sharp line, his cheekbones still defined. But no one would ever mistake him for a pretty boy. A thin scar ran under his left eye, just above the line of dark stubble on his cheek. Another one bisected the end of his right eyebrow, giving him a slightly dangerous look. *How did he get those?* she wondered.

He threw one long leg over the back of his horse and dismounted, his boots landing with a dull thud on the ground. He stood next to his mount for a second, hands still holding the reins. Then he dropped them to dangle in the dirt as he moved toward her. Isabel's heart started to pound as he drew closer. He was still tall, still broad through the shoulders. But gone was the hint of boyish softness he'd had the last time she'd seen him. Now he was long and lean, looking nicely muscled in all the right places.

He stopped about two feet away, leaving her some much-needed breathing room. "You're back," he said again. His voice was soft, with no hint of emotion. Was he happy to see her? Disappointed? Angry? Isabel searched his face for answers, but his expression was guarded, his initial surprise no longer evident.

She nodded. "Yes." Her voice sounded a little shaky even to her own ears. Not for the first time, she wished she had a better poker face. She hated the fact that she was constantly advertising her emotions.

Especially now.

Wyatt Spalding was the first man she'd ever slept with. And while he hadn't been the last, he was the only one she'd given her heart to. In hindsight, that had been a mistake. He'd wasted no time breaking it. But ten years ago, she'd been frightened and hurt. Wyatt had found her walking alone along that deserted road, the moon her only illumination. He'd wasted no time helping her, riding to her rescue in his beat-up truck like a knight of yore. She'd recognized him immediately, Diego's best friend, Wyatt. In classic younger sister fashion, she'd had a serious crush on him.

When he'd rolled up next to her and said her name, she'd felt such a wave of relief she had started crying. Misinterpreting her tears, Wyatt had climbed out of his truck and gathered her into his arms. It was the first time he'd touched her, and his embrace had felt better than any of her fantasies.

Hours later, they'd made love under the stars. Despite the pain he caused her the next day, she'd lived off the memory of their encounter for years. But out of all her experiences that fateful night, what had stuck with her the most was Wyatt's composure. He'd been calm and still while listening to her story. Diego would have flown into a rage upon hearing the details, but Wyatt had remained silent, his expression impenetrable as she'd explained what had happened.

He wore a similar look now as he eyed her up and down. "Thought you were gonna open your own practice in the big city."

Her cheeks warmed at his statement. So he remembered what she'd said all those years ago. Did that mean he still thought about her as much as she did about him?

"Things change," she said simply. She didn't want to talk about the evolution of her thinking, not when they were standing a few feet away from three dead cows. Not to mention, it wasn't the type of conversation she wanted to have after ten years of silence.

Wyatt didn't speak for a moment. He glanced up and down the fence then turned to look at the pond where the trespassing cows were still drinking. "I take it you're working for Diego now?"

Isabel bristled at the implication she took orders from her brother. "I'm working with him." Diego might be older by a few years, but that didn't make him her boss.

"When did you come back?" He wore a frown, as if he hadn't wanted to ask the question but couldn't stand not knowing the answer.

"Almost a month ago," she said. "Didn't Diego tell you?"

"I didn't ask," he replied flatly.

Well, then. Apparently she didn't cross his mind, after all.

The knowledge stung, but what could she expect? His actions the day after their encounter had showed how he'd really felt. Still, part of her had assumed that Diego had talked about her over the years, since they'd all known each other.

She pressed her lips together, hoping to hide her disappointment. "Well, here I am. Sorry my presence bothers you." She pivoted on her heel and started walking toward the dead cattle. "Thanks for bringing back our animals," she said over her shoulder. "They won't break into the park again." She was ready for him to leave, so she could return her attention to the problem at hand. It was too hard to think when he was around; his appearance had stirred up a number of emotions that were clouding her thoughts. Later, when she was alone, she'd process these feelings and what it meant to see Wyatt again. But for now, she needed to focus on the mystery of these dead animals and getting the fence repaired.

Footsteps sounded behind her. "I didn't say I was bothered." His voice made the muscles in her shoulders tighten. *Take the hint*, she thought irritably. *Get back on your horse and ride off into the sunset.*

But he kept walking, his long legs making short work of the distance between them. "Do you need some help fixing the fen…" His words trailed off at the sight of the dead cows. "Damn," he said, whistling softly. "What happened here?"

"I'm not sure yet," she murmured. Isabel knelt next to one of the animals, running her gaze over the slightly distended belly. *Not dead too long, then*, she figured. Decomposition was still setting in, which meant these cattle had likely died sometime in the night.

She felt a rustle of air as Wyatt crouched down beside her. "Doesn't look like a cougar," he remarked.

"No," she replied absently. She tried to ignore him so she could think; her brain whirred with possible explanations as she attempted to figure out what had caused three healthy-looking animals to drop dead more or less simultaneously.

The answer was there, floating around in her subconscious. She closed her eyes, trying to block out all distractions. If she could just clear her mind, she could solve this riddle. But seeing Wyatt had left her feeling flustered and being so close to him now didn't help. He wasn't talking to her or even touching her, but she was hyper aware of his breathing and of his subtle movements as he shifted to keep his balance next to her.

Disgusted with her lack of focus, Isabel opened her eyes. To her surprise, Wyatt was no longer next to her. She glanced around, wondering where he'd gone. She hadn't heard his horse, so it was unlikely he'd taken off. Besides, he surely would have said something before leaving. They might not be on the best of terms, but he wasn't a total jerk.

Isabel got to her feet, leaning down to brush the dirt off her knees. Then she turned around and spied Wyatt walking toward Miel.

The mare shifted in response to Wyatt's approach, her ears going back and her tail twitching with agitation as she assessed this new person. Isabel set off for the pair, wanting to reassure her horse that all was well. She was already jumpy—she didn't need the stress of a stranger to add to her discomfort.

But Isabel needn't have worried. Wyatt moved slowly, extending one hand for Miel to sniff. As Isabel got closer, she could hear him speaking to the horse. His voice was too low for her to make out what he was saying, but his tone was calm and his cadence measured. The mare's ears relaxed and her tail stilled; they had apparently become friends. Wyatt was patting her neck gently when Isabel walked up.

"What's her name?" he asked.

"Miel," she replied, reaching up to stroke the horse's cheek with the back of her fingers.

He smiled, his teeth a bright flash amid the dark stubble on his face. "That means 'honey,' doesn't it?" Isabel nodded. He glanced back at the horse. "Well, you certainly seem sweet enough for that name."

Wyatt moved toward her saddlebags. "What are you doing?" she asked, mildly irritated he had approached her mount without asking and now seemed intent on rifling through her packs.

"I figured you have some supplies in here. I was going to see about the fence."

"Oh." Some of her annoyance faded. "I don't have enough for a full repair."

He peered into one of the bags. "That's okay," he said, taking stock of the contents. "I've got some rope in my pack. Between the two of us, we can get this hole patched until you guys have time to fix it."

"You don't need to worry about it," she said. It was a nice gesture on his part, but she didn't need him to hang around any longer. "Diego is on his way with supplies and some extra hands. We've got it covered."

Wyatt nodded in acknowledgment, but made no move to go to his horse.

The low hum of an approaching engine sounded. "That'll be them," she said, relief filling her. "I appreciate your help, but you can get back to what you were doing now."

Wyatt's eyes glinted with amusement as he looked at her. "By my count, that's the third time you've tried to get rid of me. Are you that offended by my company?"

No, just heartsick, she thought. She'd known that by coming back to work on the family ranch she would eventually run into Wyatt. But she had assumed she'd have some advance warning before actually seeing him again. This out-of-the-blue encounter had left her no time to prepare her heart for the shock.

She glanced away with a shrug, trying to hide her face. "I figured you have park ranger things to do," she said, watching her brother's truck as it drew closer. "I don't want you to feel like you have to stay on my account."

"It's no imposition," Wyatt said. Movement from the corner of her eyes revealed he'd walked back to Miel's head and was stroking her cheek. "Besides, I need to talk to your brother."

"I see."

She set off toward the declivity, gesturing for Diego to pull the truck by the downed cattle. He backed into place, then cut the engine and climbed out of the cab.

After meeting her at the rear of the truck, Diego put his hands on his hips as he surveyed the scene, his gaze landing first on the cattle then on the break in the fence. "Well, hell," he said disgustedly. "This is the last thing we need right now."

"Yeah," Isabel acknowledged. She nodded at Ruben, one of the older, more experienced ranch hands, who'd been with them as long as she could remember. He touched the brim of his hat then turned his head to spit tobacco juice. The man never said much, but he had a way with the animals that had proved invaluable on more than one occasion.

Wyatt walked over. Diego's face lit up at the sight of his friend. "Hey, man," he said. In a standard male greeting, the pair shook hands and slapped each other's backs. "What are you doing here?"

Wyatt nodded at Ruben, who nodded back. Then he returned his focus to Diego. "Found some of your cattle in the park," he said. "Didn't really feel like doing paperwork today, so I drove 'em back to you and found the fence down and your sister standing by some dead cows."

Diego glanced at Isabel. She shrugged.

"Thanks for giving us a break," Diego replied. "It's been a rough couple of months."

Winter feed prices had gone up, and meat prices had gone down. The ranch wasn't making the same kinds of profits it had enjoyed during its heyday, and if the trend continued, they were in for some hard choices in the years to come. Isabel thought they could weather the storm if they made a few changes, but Diego wasn't so certain. It was a point of contention they would have to settle, as they were set to inherit equal shares of the ranch once their *abuelo* died.

Wyatt and Diego continued to chat as the three men worked to remove a new fence panel from the truck bed. She tried to help, but Ruben waved her off with a nod for her efforts. Within a matter of minutes, they had the new section in place and secured to the posts.

"What do you think happened here?" Diego asked as he returned to survey the cows once more.

"I'm not sure yet," Isabel admitted. "I'll open them up tonight and see if I can get some answers."

"Do you think it was deliberate?" Wyatt asked.

The question made her frown. "You think someone targeted these animals?" she asked.

He shrugged. "I think you have to consider the possibility. That fence didn't break down because of age. Someone cut it."

A tingle shot down Isabel's spine. "Sabotage."

Diego's lips blanched as he pressed them into a thin line. "Could be."

Isabel turned back to the dead animals, seeing the scene in a new light. "I assumed these two events—" she gestured to the cows and the now-repaired fence "—were simply a coincidence. We've had hikers cut the fence before to gain access to our watering holes. And it's not unheard of for cattle to die while out at pasture. It never occurred to me that someone might have broken onto the ranch to kill our animals."

"Maybe I'm being paranoid," Wyatt admitted. "There are no obvious signs of trauma here, and I doubt someone who went to the trouble of dispatching these animals with such subtlety would leave a gaping hole in the fence."

"Unless they're trying to send a message," Diego suggested.

Wyatt shrugged. "Who have you pissed off lately?"

Diego tipped his hat back and shot him a grin. "The list is long and distinguished."

Ruben spit into the dirt again. "We're losing daylight. Let's get this done."

The pronouncement had the intended effect. They set aside conversation and got to work securing chains around the downed animals' legs. That done, Diego flipped on the winch secured to the bed of his truck. The motor groaned a bit as, one by one, the bodies of the cows were lifted off the ground. The three men maneuvered them onto the flatbed and then used ropes to tie them down.

When they were finished, both Diego and Wyatt removed their hats and wiped their foreheads. "Thanks, man," Diego said.

"Anytime," Wyatt replied.

"It's getting late," Diego noted. "Why don't you come back to the house? Join us for dinner."

Isabel's breath hitched and she made a show of checking the ropes securing the cattle to the truck so Wyatt wouldn't see her face. *Please say no…*

"That's a tempting offer," Wyatt said slowly. "But I've got a bit of a ride to get back home."

"You can stay with us," Diego pressed. "We'll take care of you both for the night." He jerked his

chin in the direction of Wyatt's horse, who was placidly grazing on a clump of grass. "It's the least we
can do for all your help today."

"You don't owe me anything for that," Wyatt muttered. Isabel watched from the corner of her eyes
as he looked down, scuffing the toe of his boot in
the dirt.

His hesitation spoke volumes. It was clear Wyatt
didn't want to be around her. Unfortunately, Diego
was too clueless to notice.

"Come on," he said. "Maria will be happy to see
you. It's been ages."

Wyatt looked up, smiling faintly. "She does make
the best tortillas."

"Then it's settled," Diego announced. "Saddle up.
You and Isabel can ride back to the house together."

Isabel felt her shoulders tighten but said nothing.
Diego didn't know about her personal history with
Wyatt. If she appeared at all unhappy about her new
riding partner, her brother would want to know why.
And that wasn't an issue she was willing to discuss.

Sensing the guys were waiting for her to respond,
Isabel schooled her features and turned around.
"Let's get going then," she said. "I'm hungry."

Something's off here…

Wyatt rode alongside Isabel, watching her in his
peripheral vision. He was lucky Ajax was such a
sure-footed horse, as he was paying little attention to

the path. It was clear Isabel was unhappy about his presence, and Wyatt wanted to know why.

Ten years ago he'd found her walking along a deserted road, trying to make her way home after her boyfriend had taken her to a party in the desert and then ignored her to shack up with a willing girl. Never one to be passive, Isabel had simply started walking home rather than ask anyone for a ride. Looking back on it, Wyatt figured that was probably just as well, since all the kids there had been too drunk to drive. Still, at the time, he'd been angry with her for setting off alone into the desert.

Wyatt wasn't much for sentiment, but there were times he could still feel the weight of her head on his chest and the wetness on his skin from her tears soaking through his shirt. He rubbed his sternum with one hand, his mind wandering down memory lane...

The night air was cool on his face as he cruised down the road, the rumble of the truck engine drowning out the cricket chirps and the occasional scream of a mountain lion. Wyatt's body ached from the day's labors, but it was a good type of exhaustion, the kind that only comes from sustained physical work. It had taken all day, but now his grandfather's house sported a fresh coat of paint and the worn shutters had been replaced. It looked like a brand-new house, one they could both be proud to call home.

"Are you really going out?" his grandfather had asked, seeing him showered and dressed a few minutes ago. "I figured you'd be tired after all that work."

Wyatt had shrugged. "Some friends of mine are catching a movie tonight. Thought I'd join them." If he was lucky, he'd get there before it started. If he was really lucky, he could convince Nikki Stalling to skip the movie altogether in favor of some one-on-one time. They'd dated briefly in high school and now that they were both in college, they had a sort of on-again, off-again arrangement during school breaks. With the fall semester starting up in a few weeks, there wouldn't be many more opportunities to spend time together.

His grandfather had smiled knowingly. "I see. Well, have fun and be safe about it."

"Will do."

The road into town was just another two-lane dusty highway, the traffic nonexistent. Wyatt reached for the radio dial, his hand freezing in place when his headlights illuminated a figure walking along the side of the road. The long, dark braid and slender shoulders told him it was a woman. He slowed his truck and as he approached, his heart leaped into his throat.

It was Isabel Cruz. His best friend's sister.

She glanced over as he pulled up alongside, but didn't stop walking. Wyatt leaned over and cranked down the passenger-side window. "Isabel?" he called. "What are you doing out here?"

Her head whipped around, dark eyes going wide. "Wyatt? Is that you?"

He cut the engine as she lunged for the door. She climbed up into the cab, bringing the scent of night air and jasmine with her. He inhaled deeply, trying not to be too obvious about it. He loved her perfume—always had. For the past several months he'd been wanting to dip his nose into the hollow of her neck and breathe her in, to hold her until her scent was on his skin and clothes. But that wasn't something he could ever admit, to her or to her brother. Diego would kill him if he knew Wyatt had been thinking about Isabel in anything other than a platonic context.

"What are you doing out here?" he repeated. He hadn't seen any signs of a stalled car—where had she come from?

"I'm walking home."

He didn't bother replying to her ridiculous statement. He simply stared her down, one brow arched to show he wasn't going to give up that easily.

Isabel held his gaze for several seconds. Then she sighed and looked away. "I was at a party, okay?"

"Out in the middle of nowhere?"

She shot him an incredulous look. "Don't try to tell me you didn't go to your share of desert parties in high school, okay? I know for a fact you and Diego were regulars."

"Yeah, but..." He paused, thinking back to those days. He and Diego had had their share of fun, it was true. But Wyatt knew the kind of stuff that went on at those parties, and he didn't like the thought of Isabel being exposed to such debauchery.

Her eyes glinted with challenge, practically daring him to argue with her. He lifted one shoulder in a shrug. "It was different for us. We're guys."

She snorted. "Oh, please. I'm not some princess who needs to be locked in a tower."

"I never said you were," he replied, careful to keep his tone even. "But you're a beautiful young woman. There are guys who would try to take advantage of you."

A haunted look flashed across her face and Wyatt's stomach dropped. Oh God, he thought, immediately assuming the worst.

Before he could ask her another question, Isabel spoke again. "You think I'm beautiful?" There was a note of wonder in her voice, combined with an innocence that made her even more appealing.

Wyatt felt his cheeks warm and was grateful the lights from his dash didn't provide much illumination in the cab of the truck. "You know you're pretty," he said a bit gruffly. It was clear from Isabel's tone of voice that she hadn't been fishing for compliments. But if they kept going down this road, he wasn't going to be able to hide his attraction for her much longer.

Time to change the subject. "What happened?"

She shifted, looked away. "Nothing," she muttered.

Wyatt ran his eyes over her body, looking for marks on her skin or ripped or dirty spots on her clothes. She didn't look like she'd been assaulted, but that was no guarantee...

Anger and fear built in his chest as he imagined the worst. "Isabel." He said her name softly, trying to keep his emotions in check. If someone had hurt her, the last thing he wanted to do was to frighten her with his temper.

She didn't look at him right away. He said her name a second time and she turned to face him. His heart cracked when he saw the tears welling in her eyes.

"Oh, honey. What happened?" He opened his arms and she slid across the bench seat into his embrace.

She sniffled into his shirt, her nose pressed against his chest. "Nothing," came her muffled reply.

Wyatt kept his touch light as he gently stroked his hand down her spine. "Sounds like a lot of tears over nothing," he said carefully. "Who were you with tonight?"

Another sniffle then the muffled sound of a name. "Eddie."

His hand stilled on her back, fingers curling into a fist. He should have known.

He took a deep breath, slipping a tight rein onto his anger. Isabel deserved better than that future frat *boy. Wyatt had always considered him a harmless nuisance, but what if he'd been wrong?*

"Did Eddie—" He had to stop, swallow hard. "Did Eddie hurt you?"

Isabel tensed. Time seemed to slow as he waited for her to reply.

She moved back, putting some distance between them. "No," she said finally. "Not in the way you're thinking."

Wyatt's breath gusted out in a sigh of relief. He lifted a hand to run through his hair, noting with faint surprise that it was shaking.

Isabel grabbed it, her fingers still cold from the evening air. "I'm fine," she said, her voice firm.

He met her eyes, still wet from her tears. There was no sign of deception in her gaze. "Would you tell me if you weren't?" It was important that she knew she could trust him. She and Diego loved each other, but their relationship was tumultuous at times. Wyatt wanted her to know he would be there for her if she ever needed anything.

She didn't hesitate. "Yes," she said, nodding as she spoke. "I think I would."

He relaxed a bit, feeling marginally better. "Okay. So what did Eddie do to make you cry tonight?"

Isabel tilted her head. "Who's asking? You? Or you and Diego?"

"Just me. We don't tell each other everything, you know." Like the fact that I want you…

Isabel nodded, apparently satisfied with his reac-

tion. "It's the last big party of the summer. We came to hang out. We were having fun, but as the night wore on, more and more people started pairing up and sneaking off for some privacy. Eddie thought we should, too, but..." She trailed off, shaking her head. "I kept saying no."

A feeling of pride unfurled in Wyatt's chest. Thank God, Isabel wasn't a pushover. "How'd he take it?" Given the kid's sense of entitlement, Wyatt didn't imagine Eddie had been too happy about her refusal.

Tears welled in her eyes again. Wyatt swore silently to himself. Eddie wasn't worth her tears. But that was something she was going to have to learn on her own.

"He was mad," she said. "He kept pressuring me, and when I told him to stop or I was going to leave, he laughed. Told me I was welcome to try."

Eddie was an idiot. But Wyatt was glad to learn he wasn't stupid enough to force himself on her.

She sniffed, swiping at her eyes with a hand. "Then he wandered away and grabbed Carrie Cordova. They started making out by the campfire, and I wasn't about to stand around and be disrespected like that."

She glanced up and met his gaze, and a small shock ran through Wyatt's body as he realized she wasn't crying because she was sad.

She was angry.

"He had his keys in his pocket. I thought about trying to hot-wire his car, but I only saw Diego do *it the one time to the farm truck. I don't exactly re-member how."*

Wyatt tried not to smile as he imagined Isabel fumbling under the wheel of Eddie's prize Camaro. "I hate to break it to you, but a muscle car is a lit-tle harder to hot-wire than a thirty-year-old truck." She would have kept at it and, given her determina-tion, she might have even figured it out eventually. Probably better she'd started walking, though. Ed-die's parents were just the type to have her charged with grand theft auto if she'd managed to make off with their precious son's car.

"I'll teach you how to do it," he promised ab-sently. Now that he knew she was safe, annoyance began to replace his earlier concern.

"You should have called someone to pick you up."

Isabel dug her phone out of her bag. "No service." She held it up in illustration. It was a common prob-lem out here, something that normally didn't bother him. It worried him, though, to think about her es-sentially stranded out here.

"Why didn't you drive yourself out there to begin with?" There was an edge to his voice that was ob-vious even to him.

Isabel lifted one brow. "Because I didn't see the need to take two cars when we were both going to the same place."

"Leaving you at the mercy of Eddie's whims." Wyatt shook his head. "That wasn't very smart of you."

"I don't recall asking you." She spoke softly, but Wyatt knew she wouldn't stay quiet for long. He recognized the set of her mouth—it was the same expression Diego wore right before he lost his temper.

He knew he should stop, but he just couldn't help himself. "What were you thinking, walking out here alone?"

"I needed to leave. There were no other options," she said evenly.

"And what if someone else had found you? Someone without my good intentions?" Why was she being so stubborn? Didn't she realize the kind of danger she'd been in?

She lifted one shoulder in a shrug. "I can handle myself."

He scoffed. "Is that right?"

"Yeah. I have pepper spray in my bag."

Wyatt's anger took over. Without pausing to think, he grabbed her wrist and hauled her close, holding her against his chest. She barely had time to let out a squeak of surprise before he tilted his body, pressing her back flat onto the bench seat. In the next breath he shifted his legs so they tangled with hers. He gripped her free hand then lifted both arms above her head. Her wrists fit easily into his palm, leaving him with one hand free.

She was pinned underneath him, immobile and totally at his mercy.

"How's that pepper spray working out for you

now?" The words were barely more than a growl in the back of his throat.

Isabel tested his hold, making a small sound of frustration when he didn't loosen his grip. She shifted under him, the movement only serving to emphasize the contact between their bodies. Wyatt immediately realized his mistake; if she kept this up much longer, she was going to learn an entirely different type of lesson.

She stilled against him but didn't fully relax. He met her gaze, saw the question in her eyes.

His heart started to thump hard against his sternum. Was he imagining things, or did Isabel want him the same way he wanted her?

As much as he'd like to hope his feelings for her were mutual, this was not the way he should be treating the sister of his best friend. He gave her wrists a squeeze then released her.

Shame was a cold stone in his stomach as he watched Isabel from the corner of his eye. She sat up, smoothed a hand over her shirt. The silence in the cab grew until it seemed to take up all the space between them.

Way to go, he told himself. If Isabel was attracted to him, he'd gone and wrecked any chance he might have had with her with that little stunt.

He pulled the seat belt over his chest and fastened it at his hip. Then he turned the key in the ignition. "I'll take you home," he said quietly.

"No."

He turned his head so quickly he nearly gave himself whiplash. "What?"

"I said no." There was no inflection in her voice. She stared ahead, her gaze focused on something beyond the windshield.

A wave of nausea washed over Wyatt. God, he'd really done it now. He should have never touched her like that. It was clear she was disgusted by him, and rightly so.

"Isabel," he croaked. "I'm sorry. I won't come near you again. But I can't leave you here to walk home by yourself."

She glanced at him then, her expression inscrutable. "I'm not asking you to leave me. And I'm not mad at you. I just don't want to go home."

Wyatt felt some of the tension leave his body as he realized she didn't hate him. "Where do you want to go?"

Isabel tilted her head to the side, causing a strand of dark hair to fall across her face. He resisted the urge to brush it behind her ear. After the way he'd pinned her down, he didn't deserve to touch her.

"Can we just drive around for a bit?" she asked. "It'd be nice to talk."

"Talk?" he echoed.

"Yeah." She nodded, her mind apparently made up. "If you don't have any plans, that is."

"No." The image of Nikki's face floated through his brain, a distraction he immediately dismissed.

He'd rather spend time with Isabel than see a thousand movies with Nikki.

Isabel gave him a small smile, setting his heart alight. He tipped his hat in her direction and her smile blossomed into a grin. "All right," he said softly, shifting the truck into gear. "Let's go."

"Let's go."

Isabel's voice cut through Wyatt's reverie. He shook himself free of the memories and realized they were nearly to the ranch's stables. "I'm sorry, what did you say?" He'd been so distracted by the past he wasn't sure what Isabel wanted him to do.

She eyed him with exasperation. "I said we have an empty stall toward the back. You can put your horse there for the night."

They arrived at the stables in question. Wyatt dismounted, but Isabel remained astride Miel. She jerked her chin in the direction of the shadowed interior. "Last box on the left. One of the hands will be along shortly to help you."

"What about you?"

"I'm going to find Diego. I don't want him putting those carcasses in the barn."

"I could help you." He moved to get back on Ajax, but Isabel shook her head.

"No need. Just see to your horse and then let yourself inside the house. Maria will give you something to drink."

He nodded. It was clear Isabel wanted to dismiss him, so he decided to play along.

"Thanks," he said. "I appreciate it."

"No problem." She shifted the reins, turning Miel's head so they could ride off. "Thanks for your help today," she said over her shoulder.

He watched her depart, his curiosity more heightened than ever. The past decade had offered no answers as to Isabel's sudden change toward him. But now that she was back, he had an opportunity to find out why she'd cut him off with no explanation.

She'd been silent long enough. It was time for her to answer his questions.

Chapter 3

"Not there!" Isabel shouted to be heard over the rumble of the truck's engine. She waved her arms for good measure, catching the attention of Ruben. The older man touched Diego's arm and her brother glanced in the rearview mirror and saw her standing outside.

He rolled down his window. "What's the problem?" He sounded annoyed, and with good reason. The day was drawing to a close and there was still a lot of work to be done.

"I don't want you to put them in the barn. If they died from some kind of disease, the pathogen might contaminate the place. The last thing we need is to have new moms and their calves exposed."

Diego pressed his lips together. "Okay, so where do you want them?"

Isabel considered her options. It would be easier for her to work indoors, but it would be difficult to drag the carcasses inside. Besides, there wasn't a good building where she could do this kind of work. The barn was reserved for cows that were having trouble calving, and the stables housed the horses. Neither site met her needs.

The easiest thing would be to conduct the necropsy outside. She could collect the necessary tissue samples and the carcasses could then be dragged off for burial or burned in place.

Her mind made up, she instructed Diego to drop the bodies off in a clearing about fifty yards away from the barn. The wide patch of dirt would give her space to work, and if the area did become contaminated with some kind of pathogen, the lack of grass meant the other animals wouldn't be nosing around the site tomorrow. It wasn't a perfect setup, but it would have to do.

She led Miel to the spot then dismounted and stood back while Diego and Ruben emerged from the truck. The two men removed the ropes securing the carcasses to the flatbed. With the push of a button, one end of the bed lifted, putting the flat slab at an angle. While Ruben coiled the rope, Diego climbed back into the truck and slowly moved it forward. The three dead cows slid off and landed with a thump. A second later, a foul smell tinged the air.

Miel danced in place. Diego emerged from the truck and wrinkled his nose. "Dear God. That's terrible."

Isabel shrugged. "Could be worse. They haven't been dead long enough to really stink."

Diego shook his head. "If you say so."

"Can you take Miel to the stables for me?" She should have left her there when she'd dropped off Wyatt. But she'd needed to get away, to put some distance between herself and the man who'd broken her heart all those years ago.

"I'll take her," Ruben said quietly.

"Thanks." Isabel smiled at him. "I should get changed."

Diego clapped her on the shoulder. "We'll leave you to it." She could tell by the gleam in his eyes that he was all too happy to have her handle the messy task ahead.

"Thanks," she drawled. The men began to leave, Diego turning back to his truck and Ruben heading toward Miel. "Gentlemen," Isabel called out, stopping them in their tracks.

Diego lifted his eyebrows in an unspoken question. "I'm probably being paranoid," she said, glancing down at the cattle. "But make sure you wash up. If you start to feel sick in the next few days, let me know immediately." If these animals had died from an infectious disease, there was a small chance it could be passed on to them. But hopefully that wasn't the case…

"Will do," her brother said. Ruben merely touched the brim of his hat in acknowledgment.

Isabel studied the inert trio at her feet then glanced up at the sky. There was probably one good hour of daylight left before dusk began to set in. She'd have to hurry.

Ten minutes later, she walked out the door of the big ranch house clad in ratty old scrubs and a worn pair of rubber shoes. Tilting her head down, she reached for her hair and set to work resecuring her ponytail. She skipped down the porch stairs, drawing up short as a pair of boots entered her vision.

Still working on her hair, she stepped to the right. The boots mirrored her movements, blocking her path once more. There were only two people on this ranch who would deliberately try to irritate her, and those weren't her brother's boots.

Sure enough, she lifted her gaze to find Wyatt standing in front of her. She could tell by his expression he wanted to talk to her, but she didn't have time for a conversation right now.

"Excuse me," she said, stepping to the side. When he matched her movements again, she narrowed her eyes.

He lifted one hand to stave off her response. "I'm here to help you."

"Is that right?" She considered the possibility. It was doubtful he'd ever participated in the necropsy of a cow before, but he was strong and there was a lot of lifting and shifting involved. Still, was the convenience of his assistance worth the price in distraction she'd have to pay?

"You have three animals to examine, and from what I understand, the process isn't exactly fast. You said you were hungry earlier. I assume you're not going to eat until you're done with the cows?"

"No," she confirmed. The longer she waited to gather samples, the less chance they'd be useful. "I need to take care of this first."

"So let me help you." When she didn't immediately accept his offer, he pointed to the sky. "You're running out of daylight. I know you're not happy to see me, but let's put aside our differences and get this done."

He was right, and the practical part of her brain knew it. Even though he wasn't a skilled veterinary assistant, the process would still go considerably faster with him there.

"Okay." She nodded. "But we need to get you some protection first."

"Protection?" he echoed. There was a note of concern in his voice, as though he might be rethinking this plan.

"This is a messy job," she said, hiding a smile. "Wouldn't want to get blood and gore all over your pretty uniform." His dark green pants would probably fare all right, but his khaki shirt would be ruined. "Plus, I'm not sure what killed these animals. We need to be careful in case it's some kind of infection."

He nodded, but she saw his Adam's apple bob as he swallowed. "Lead the way."

A grudging respect bubbled up inside her chest as Isabel took them to the barn. Wyatt wasn't any more excited to spend time with her than she was to see him, but he was willing to put aside his annoyance to help her get this done in a timely manner. And he was willing to take on the risk that the process would expose him to a pathogen. It was a small chance, but a consideration nonetheless.

If he could act like an adult, so could she. It would be much more emotionally satisfying to ignore him, but that wasn't going to get this job done. Besides, since she was now living and working on the family ranch again, she was bound to run into Wyatt from time to time. They were going to have to find a way to tolerate each other, for Diego's sake. Might as well start working on that now.

It didn't take long to gather her supplies. Arms laden with gear, she and Wyatt trudged over to the downed cattle. Once there, she handed him some plastic coveralls and a mask, along with two plastic bags for his shoes.

"Step into these and tie the loops around your ankles," she advised. "Blood doesn't come out of boots."

"Speaking from experience?"

"Unfortunately, yes," she said.

"That's a rather ominous observation," he said,

sliding one sack over his left boot. "Good thing I know you're a vet."

She smiled as she donned her own set of coveralls. "Here's another troubling piece of advice—put a lot of Vicks under your nose. Otherwise, the smell of death is going to get into your sinuses, and you'll be living with it for days."

"Lovely," he said dryly.

"It's not too late to back out," she said.

Wyatt shook his head. "Nope. I said I'd help and I will."

Isabel nodded. "Then let's get started."

She conducted an external exam of the first animal, looking for signs of injury she'd initially missed. Nothing jumped out, so she picked up her knife and began the dissection.

Wyatt remained quiet, responding quickly to her requests to hold this leg, hand her that vial. The first thing she noticed as she worked was the color of the animal's muscles—they'd gone from the normal red to a dark grayish shade. That might be an important clue, or it may simply be due to the fact the animals had been dead for several hours.

She continued to work, cutting through tissue and moving organs. Blood began to pool in the crevices and hollows she exposed, another strange finding.

"I'm no expert, but I thought dead animals don't bleed," Wyatt said quietly.

"They don't," she replied shortly. "At least, they're not supposed to." Normally, clotting occurred shortly after death. It wasn't unusual to find fluids inside deceased animals, but this level of liquid blood was outside the norm.

She filed the information away and continued her exam. The heart muscle had hemorrhaged into the surrounding space; so had the lung tissue. She turned to the rumen next, one of the four chambers of the stomach. It was already distended with gas, a combination of decay and the normal buildup of methane. The fetid air hissed around Isabel's scalpel as she made her cut. She sniffed, detecting the familiar odors of sulfur, partially digested grass and stomach acid.

But there was an additional scent that gave her pause: almonds.

The pieces suddenly clicked into place. "Cyanide," she muttered. It was the only explanation for these findings.

"Did I hear you say cyanide?"

She looked up, saw Wyatt's eyes wide above his mask. "Yes," she said. "Can't you smell it?"

He shook his head. "All I smell is rotten eggs and VapoRub. What am I missing?"

"Almonds. Not everyone can smell it. Hand me that kit, please." She dug a test tube out of the cardboard box and carefully scooped some of the rumen contents into the glass. Then she placed a strip of test paper at the top of the tube and added the cap. She gave the tube a gentle shake and watched as the yellow test strip turned a brown-orange color.

"Bingo," she said quietly.

"So it's poison?" Wyatt asked.

She collected a few more samples to send off for a definitive diagnosis. But based on what she'd seen and this test, Isabel was confident these animals had died from cyanide.

"Not necessarily," she said, moving on to the next animal. "It's not uncommon for some plants to produce cyanide as a defense mechanism. Sometimes, grazing animals ingest too much and it winds up killing them."

"Does that happen often?"

She shook her head. "It's not common, but it's not unheard of, either." She frowned as she continued her work. "The thing is, we're pretty careful to ensure we don't have a lot of cyanogenic plants around."

"Did you notice any in the spot where you found these guys?"

Isabel finished her exam of the second cow and moved to the third. It was going faster, now that she knew what to look for. "I didn't, but that doesn't mean much. I can only recognize a few of the plants by sight. I'll need to go back out there and do a more thorough search."

"I can help," Wyatt offered. "I'm pretty good with plants."

She considered his offer. "That would be great. If you really don't mind."

"Not at all."

"Don't you have to get back to rangering?" She

wasn't quite sure what his days were like; she knew he didn't punch a time clock, but surely he had some regular duties that required his presence?

He chuckled. "I radioed in and told them I was camping tonight. I'll check in again tomorrow morning. I can ride out to the site with you on my way back to the park."

"I appreciate it." She continued her work, collecting samples and recording observations. Although she was confident in her presumptive diagnosis of cyanide poisoning, she wanted to send the samples for processing all the same. There was additional information to be gleaned, such as the type of plant material in the animals' stomachs, along with the approximate concentration of toxin in their systems. All facts that would paint a fuller picture of what had happened, and help Isabel and Diego come up with strategies to ensure it didn't occur again.

The light was fading when Isabel finished her exam of the third cow. She stood, lifting her arms over her head to stretch muscles gone stiff from crouching for so long.

"What happens now?" Wyatt asked, gesturing to the gruesome scene at their feet.

Isabel took a step back and began to strip off her gloves and plastic gown. "Now we call Diego. We did the messy part. He gets to clean it up."

Wyatt pulled his mask off, revealing a grin. "Somehow, I don't think he'll like that."

She shrugged. "He'll whine about it, but it's not

a tough job. I had him put the bodies far enough away from any buildings so the disposal would be a simple matter."

"Bury or burn?" Wyatt asked.

"Burn," Isabel replied. "There's no wind tonight, and no grass nearby, either. Lighting them up is the easiest thing to do." She picked up the walkie-talkie sitting in the dirt next to the samples she'd collected.

"Diego, come in."

It took a few seconds for her brother to respond. "Yeah. What's up?"

"I'm ready for you out here. Bring the gasoline."

"Roger that."

She glanced at Wyatt, who was busy stripping off his plastic gear. "You survived your first necropsy," she remarked.

He nodded, staring at the remains with a kind of puzzled fascination, as if he couldn't quite believe what he was seeing. "I suppose I did."

"You make a good assistant," she said. "In case you need a fallback career."

One corner of his mouth twitched up in a lopsided smile that was dangerously endearing. "I think I'll stick with being a park ranger."

Isabel glanced away, determined not to fall under the spell of Wyatt's effortless charm. "I know that was always your dream." They'd talked about it, that night he'd found her. He'd told her all about his desire to be a ranger, and she'd shared her goals of becoming a veterinarian. Eddie, her boyfriend at the time, had never been terribly interested in hearing about her plans for the future. Wyatt had been the first man outside of her family who'd actually seemed to care about her ideas. His attention had given her a heady rush, better than any roller-coaster ride. Was it any wonder she'd fallen for him?

He moved closer, balling up his discarded protective gear as he walked. "It was," he said. "Just like you wanted to become a vet. I guess both our dreams came true."

She glanced at him then, felt a spark of kinship as their eyes met. "Is it everything you thought it would be?" The question tumbled out before she had a chance to think twice. What was she doing, asking him something so personal? She needed to keep him at arm's length, not invite him to share his private thoughts as to the way his life had turned out.

Except…she cared. Wyatt had always been Diego's friend, but the three of them had shared some fun times together growing up. He had been a part of her life for a long time, and even though Wyatt had broken her heart, she still worried about him, still wanted him to be happy.

It was a strange dichotomy, the way she felt. There were times when Isabel could close her eyes and be right back in the moment when she'd seen Wyatt and Nikki in a passionate clutch outside the coffee shop, not even twelve hours after he'd made love to her in the back of his truck. The shock of it had knocked the breath from her lungs, made her light-headed. She'd literally felt something give inside her chest, had needed to sit down to let the feeling pass. At the time, she didn't think she'd ever get over the pain of his betrayal.

But as the years had passed, her anger and hurt had given way to a more nuanced understanding. Wyatt had been—still was, come to that—a handsome guy. Charming, funny, smart—he was the total package. Yes, they'd slept together. But they hadn't made any promises to each other that night. She might have given him her heart, but he hadn't reciprocated. The young girl she'd once been couldn't imagine a greater pain. But the woman she'd grown to be recognized that was okay. In fact, it was probably for the best. They'd both gone their separate ways for school, her to College Station, him to Lubbock. The distance alone would have made things difficult. Besides, if they'd tried to keep a relationship alive, Diego would have had a hard time. He'd always been so protective of her, thinking no one was good enough for his little sister. She'd never want to make him choose between her and his best friend.

Given their complicated history, Isabel thought it best that she and Wyatt remain on friendly, if impersonal, terms. Asking him if his reality had lived up to his expectations definitely crossed her mental line in the sand.

In the fading afternoon light, his blue eyes held a hint of gray. "I can't complain," he said. "There are some things I don't like about my job, about my life. But the good far outweighs the bad. What about you?"

"Same," Isabel replied. She was saved from having to say more by the rumble of Diego's approaching truck.

Her brother hopped out, surveyed the scene. If he was surprised by Wyatt's presence, he didn't show it. "You two find any answers?"

"Cyanide," Isabel said. She held up her clutch of samples, the glass tubes jangling a bit against the metal rack. "I'm going to send these out for processing to confirm, but I'm positive it's cyanide."

Diego frowned. "I don't recall seeing any dangerous plants out there today."

"I'm going to check tomorrow, do a more thorough search of the area," she replied.

"I'm going to help her," Wyatt added. "I'm good with plants."

Diego nodded. "Thanks, Ranger Rick," he drawled. "Can I get your help with this, too?" He nodded in the direction of the truck bed, which held two five-gallon gasoline containers.

"I suppose," Wyatt said.

"Here." Isabel gestured for Wyatt to hand over his trash. "I'll take care of that." She gathered everything into her arms: the samples, their discarded gear, her tools. "I've got my own cleanup to do. See you both at dinner."

The men said their goodbyes, the pair already focused on spreading gas over the animal carcasses.

Isabel set off for the barn, but stopped after a few steps. She turned back, her eyes landing on Wyatt's tall form and graceful movements.

"Wyatt." At the sound of his name, he glanced up. "Thanks again for your help today."

His smile was full of warmth, drawing her in despite her desire to keep things superficial. "Any time."

She looked away before he could see the rising blush on her cheeks. *Cut it out*, she told her body as she headed back to the barn. A few hours in Wyatt's presence and her hormones were already stirring, wanting to pick things up where they'd left off ten years ago.

Not an option.

But despite her mental protests, her stomach fluttered with anticipation.

Chapter 4

"¡*Mijo!* I thought that was you!"

Wyatt smiled with genuine pleasure as he trailed into the living room after Diego. Maria, the family's long-standing housekeeper, walked out of the kitchen, wooden spoon in hand. Her lined face beamed as she smiled up at him. "How long has it been?"

"Too long," Wyatt replied, wrapping his arms around her small frame. Although he still saw Diego regularly, he hadn't been out to the house in ages. Maria didn't seem to have changed much—she sported a few more laugh lines at the corners of her eyes, a few more silver strands in her dark hair. But her warm brown eyes still glowed with affection and he felt the strength in her slender body as she gripped him tight.

She pulled back, frowning slightly. *"Mijo está muy pequeño y delgado,"* she said to Diego.

Wyatt laughed. "I'm not that thin," he protested.

Maria harrumphed, clearly unimpressed. "You boys get cleaned up. Dinner will be ready soon."

"Yes, ma'am," Wyatt said.

"You are staying the night?"

"Yes, ma'am," he repeated. "If that's all right?"

She swatted at him with the spoon. "Of course. Give me your clothes. I will wash them."

"Oh, no, Tía Maria. I couldn't possibly ask you—"

Maria put her hands on her hips and glared. "Did you ask?"

Diego snickered, but covered it with a cough when Maria turned her gaze on him.

Wyatt tried again. "It's fine, you don't need to do my laundry."

Maria ignored his protests. "You give him something to wear," she instructed Diego. "Then bring me his clothes."

"Sí, Mami," Diego said. Maria smiled at the nickname. She wasn't Diego's mother—wasn't even his grandmother. But she'd been the ranch housekeeper and cook for so many years she was a de facto member of the family.

"But—"

"Dude, just go with it," Diego muttered. "You're not gonna win this one."

Maria nodded. "Listen to him," she said. She reached up to pat Wyatt's cheek then drew her hand back. "Ouch!" she joked. "So rough."

Wyatt grabbed her hand and brought it to his mouth to press a kiss into her palm. "Sorry, Tía."

She smiled at him, her eyes going misty. "Go on now. I have work to do."

Wyatt watched her walk back to the kitchen, his heart warming at the sight. Fifteen years ago, Diego had brought him home for dinner. Maria had taken one look at him—a skinny kid with clothes that were just this side of too small—and immediately tried to feed him. For Wyatt, the experience had been a revelation. His parents had left when he was young, so he'd grown up living with his grandfather. And while the old man had always taken care of the basics—food, shelter, education—the rest had been considered luxuries. It wasn't out of stinginess on his grandfather's part; they simply couldn't afford much more than the necessities.

"Come on," Diego said, elbowing Wyatt as he walked past. "You can stay in your old room."

"Thanks," Wyatt muttered. He and Diego had spent so much time together while growing up that the guest bedroom at the ranch house had become his home away from home. Had it changed much since the last time he'd been here?

As it turned out, no. The second-floor room looked much the same, with the exception of new sheets on the bed. Diego grabbed a T-shirt and a pair of sweatpants from his own room, brought them back and handed them to Wyatt. "Go ahead and use Isabel's bathroom," he said, gesturing down the hall. "She won't be in for a bit."

Diego left him to head for his own bathroom. Wyatt toed off his boots, stripped off his socks. Then he padded down the hall and ducked into Isabel's bathroom, quietly closing the door behind him.

It felt strange, maybe even a little wrong, to be in her space without an invitation. But he needed to wash away the dust and sweat from a day spent in the saddle. Odds were Isabel wouldn't be pleased to find him there, so he needed to get in and get out before she saw him.

He flipped on the water, peeled off his clothes. The hot spray felt good on his back and shoulders. He glanced around for a bar of soap only to find several bottles lined up along a shallow shelf.

Seeing no other alternative, Wyatt reached for one. Shampoo—okay, that would work. It didn't take long to wash his hair, so he grabbed another bottle. Body wash.

All right, then.

He squirted a dollop into his palm. The smell of night-blooming jasmine filled the air, making his heart thump.

Isabel's scent.

He lathered up, rinsed off, cut the water. As he toweled dry, he caught whiffs of the heady floral that still clung to his skin. Memories of that night ten years ago rolled over him, heating his blood. The last time his skin had smelled like Isabel had been after they'd made love. They'd lain in each other's arms, their breathing in sync as they'd watched the stars move overhead. He'd been so happy, so at peace with the world and his place in it.

Wyatt had never felt such a total connection to another person before. He'd spent the past ten years chasing that feeling, trying to recapture the magic he'd experienced with Isabel. Surely there was someone else out there who could touch his soul the way Isabel had? If so, he had yet to find her.

Shaking off the memories, Wyatt pulled on the sweatpants. As soon as he examined the shirt, he knew he was in trouble. It was far too small for him. Had Diego given him one of Isabel's shirts as a joke, or by mistake? Either way, he needed another loaner. Maria would tan his hide if he came downstairs half dressed.

Wyatt opened the bathroom door, stepping out into the hall.

And very nearly collided with Isabel.

"Whoa." They both took a step back, avoiding contact. "Sorry about that," he said.

Her eyes widened as she looked him over. A wave of self-consciousness washed over Wyatt, making him feel as though he'd stepped out naked rather than simply shirtless.

Isabel swallowed, fixing her gaze deliberately on his face. "Um, do you need clothes?"

"Yeah." He held up the shirt Diego had given him. "Your brother gave me one of your T-shirts by mistake."

Isabel rolled her eyes. "It was his turn to fold the clothes last time. Come with me."

He followed her down the hall, past the second bathroom and the faint sounds of the shower running within. She pushed open the door to Diego's room and headed for the chair in the corner.

At least, Wyatt thought it was a chair. At the moment it was piled so high with socks, boxer shorts and bandannas it looked like a mountain of laundry.

Isabel started digging through the pile of clothes. "He hates folding," she explained. "So when it's his turn, he sorts everything by owner and simply piles all of his stuff in here."

"Maria lets him get away with that?" Wyatt didn't imagine the no-nonsense woman would appreciate Diego's approach to laundry.

"She doesn't touch our rooms," Isabel said. "And she's no fool. If she started folding Diego's clothes, he'd simply surrender the sorting job to her, as well. It's a classic case of feigned male incompetence."

Wyatt couldn't help but smile. "Dare I ask?"

She shot him a look as she worked. "You know what I'm talking about. You're asked to do something you don't want to do, so you do a crappy job hoping the asker will get fed up with your inability to do the task correctly. Then you get to sit back and pretend you tried to be helpful but your efforts just weren't appreciated."

"Ah." Wyatt had to admit that sounded familiar. It wasn't an approach he currently deployed, but there had been many times during his teenage years he'd tried that tactic with certain chores. "I suppose you can't blame a guy for trying?"

Isabel snorted. "If you say so." She straightened, apparently giving up on Mount Laundry. "I'm not finding any T-shirts in here. I'll just grab you something out of his closet." She opened the door, tsking at the sight of the mess within. "How does he live like this?" she muttered.

Wyatt stepped closer, curious to judge for himself. Diego's room certainly wasn't spotless, but it didn't seem too bad—just normal guy clutter. If Isabel thought her brother's room was a wreck, what would she think about Wyatt's cabin?

Doesn't matter, he told himself, accepting the plaid work shirt she offered and shrugging into it. *She'll never see it.*

"Need anything else?" she asked. Her eyes fixed on his fingers as he moved from button to button. The attention nearly made him fumble; he wasn't used to having an audience while he dressed.

Especially not a woman.

He watched her face as he fastened the shirt. There was an emotion in her eyes he couldn't quite identify—banked desire, perhaps? Or was that simply his imagination, seeing things that weren't really there?

She leaned forward and reached up, flipping out the collar of the shirt. He caught her gaze as she lowered her hands. Her breath hitched, brown eyes shining as she looked into his face.

The air grew thick between them. Wyatt felt the faint stirrings of that old magic as the tip of her tongue darted out to moisten her lips.

"Isabel?" he whispered. Her name was part question, part plea. What was happening here? And did she feel it, too?

He felt himself leaning in, as if pulled toward her by some invisible force. His heart thumped hard when she angled her head, moving slightly closer to him.

"What's a guy gotta do for some privacy?"

Diego's voice made Isabel jump. A guilty expression flashed across her face before she turned to her brother. "If you wanted privacy, maybe you should have given Wyatt a shirt that fit him in the first place."

Diego frowned, rubbing his hair with a towel. "What are you talking about?"

Wyatt reached for the T-shirt, snagging it off the top of the pile of laundry. "This belongs to your sister."

"Oh." Diego shrugged, as if this type of mistake happened all the time. "My bad."

"Got any more of my clothes in here?" Isabel asked, making her way to the door.

"I don't think so, but feel free to look." Diego tossed the one towel onto his bed while holding another around his waist, and started rummaging, picking out a pair of boxers and some socks. "It would probably be easiest if you folded stuff while you searched. You know, to help you figure out what you'd already looked at and what remains to be examined."

"I'll pass, thanks." Isabel's voice was cotton-candy sweet. She shot Wyatt a look as she walked out of the room. He smothered a smile. Feigned male incompetence, indeed.

"Are you really so lazy you can't fold your own clothes?"

Diego shrugged, yanking his boxers into place under the towel he wore around his waist. He tossed that towel to join the first on the bed. "It's boring," he replied. "And I've got enough to do already."

"You think your sister doesn't?"

Diego eyed him thoughtfully as he pulled a shirt from his closet. "She does," he replied. "But she and Maria seem to be the only ones who care if my clothes are folded. If it bothers her that much, she's welcome to do something about it."

"Fair enough." Wyatt headed for the door, intending to give his friend the privacy he'd requested.

"Since when did you care about Isabel's schedule, anyway?"

It was an innocent question, but Wyatt heard the subtle note of challenge.

"I don't." He stopped at the doorway, glanced back with a shrug. "Just giving you a hard time, man."

Diego grinned. "Yeah, well, I've seen your place. You don't have a lot of room to talk."

"It's not that bad." Wyatt lived in housing provided for Big Bend employees, which amounted to a small cabin in Panther Junction, a complex in the middle of the park. It wasn't fancy, but it held the essentials and kept the rain out. Things were a bit dusty and he could probably stand to sweep the floors more often, but overall Wyatt liked his little home.

"Whatever you say, brother." Diego turned his attention back to getting dressed. Wyatt returned to the guest room and stepped into his boots. Then he set off down the hall, heading for the stairs. Maria would never let him help in the kitchen, but he intended to make the offer nevertheless.

He passed Isabel's bathroom. The door was shut, the sound of running water coming from within. He caught another whiff of her bath gel, had to force himself to keep moving. If Diego found him standing outside his sister's bathroom sniffing the air, he'd start asking questions that Wyatt didn't want to answer.

Turning his thoughts back to the events of the day and away from the subject of Isabel in the shower, Wyatt walked downstairs. As soon as his boots hit the ground floor, Maria peered around the doorway to the dining room. She glanced from one empty hand to the other, narrowing her eyes.

"*Mijo*, what did I say?"

Wyatt felt his cheeks warm and wanted to disappear into the floor. He'd only been there half an hour, but Maria already had him feeling like a kid again.

"I was hoping you'd forgotten."

The look she gave him was pure contempt. She muttered something in Spanish that he figured he was better off not hearing.

"No olvido nada." I don't forget anything.

Feeling sufficiently chastened, Wyatt ran a hand through his hair. *"Sí,* Tía Maria. I'll go get them now."

"Told you you weren't going to win this one." Diego appeared behind him, carrying Wyatt's clothes. "Here you go, Mami."

Maria's face brightened. "Thank you. Be a good boy and put them in the washer for me. I've got to stir the beans." She disappeared into the kitchen, leaving Diego holding the clothes and wearing a bewildered expression.

"How did I get stuck doing your laundry?" he grumbled.

Wyatt laughed. "She played you. Here, give them to me. I'll take them back upstairs."

"Oh no." Diego shook his head. "If I don't wash them, there will be hell to pay."

"At least let me help."

"Works for me."

It didn't take long to start the process, and after the machine was humming, they wandered back into the living room and over to the kitchen, drawn by the delicious smells wafting through the air. Despite his earlier joking, Diego told him he'd finish up the laundry later.

They paused at the entrance to the kitchen, both men having learned through years of experience that Maria did not appreciate unauthorized incursions into her domain.

"It smells wonderful," Wyatt said.

"Anything we can do to help?" Diego asked.

She shot them a smile before turning her attention back to the stove, where something bubbled in a saucepan. "No, thank you. I will call if I need anything. Go visit your *abuelo*. See if you can get him to stop working."

Diego nudged Wyatt's arm, indicating he should follow. "Your grandfather still works outside?" He couldn't believe it—Jose had to be pushing eighty years old by now. Surely he no longer labored in the heat?

Diego shook his head. "He stays inside most days. Maria's orders."

"I wouldn't want to cross her," Wyatt said.

"He had a bit of a scare a few years ago," Diego continued. "Heat exhaustion. The doctors said he was lucky. Given his age, things could have gone a lot differently. Ever since then, Maria has insisted he stay inside and leave the manual work to the rest of us."

"Seems fair," Wyatt said.

"Oh, absolutely," replied Diego. "But try getting him to agree."

They arrived at the study. Diego rapped his knuckles on one side of the sliding doors, which were closed. *"Pasa,"* came the muted reply.

Diego entered first, with Wyatt trailing behind. The room looked much as it had the last time Wyatt had been inside—bookshelves lined three walls, with the fourth dominated by a large picture window that let in the sun and provided a nice view of the pastures that extended from the back of the house. A large desk sat under the window and, from this angle, Wyatt could see it was covered in ledgers and notebooks, with a few loose papers strewed about for good measure.

"Diego, why do I smell burned meat?"

"We found three animals down today," Diego replied.

His grandfather swiveled around in his chair to face them. "Three?" He noticed Wyatt standing by Diego and smiled at him. "Wyatt! *¡Que bueno verte!*"

"It's good to see you, too." Wyatt stepped forward to shake the old man's hand.

"You're staying for dinner?"

"Yes, sir," Wyatt replied.

"Good, good. Maria will be happy to have someone new at the table. I'm afraid the three of us are no longer interesting."

Wyatt smiled. "I doubt that, sir." Diego's grandfather had an amazing history. His grandparents had moved north out of Mexico shortly after the Texas Revolution. They'd settled on this land and built a cattle ranch, one that the Cruz family had owned and operated ever since. Jose Cruz had inherited the ranch from his parents, and since his own son had passed away some twenty years ago, when the time came, Diego and Isabel would take over.

Jose waved away Wyatt's words, turning his attention back to his grandson. "What happened to them?"

"Isabel says it was cyanide."

Jose frowned, his warm brown eyes narrowing. He made a thoughtful sound from low in his throat and leaned back in the chair. "We've always had trouble with Johnson grass. And we did have that cold snap a few weeks ago," he said softly. It was clear he was thinking out loud, puzzling over possibilities.

"You're thinking the weather stressed out the Johnson grass, made it produce toxic levels of cyanide?" Wyatt asked.

"Maybe," Jose replied. "What does Isabel think?"

"She agrees," a familiar feminine voice stated.

Wyatt turned as Isabel stepped into the room. She walked over to kiss Jose on the cheek. "Though I'm not sure it's Johnson grass that's our culprit. I don't recall seeing any in that spot."

"Wouldn't take a lot to kill, if there was a build up of cyanide," Diego pointed out. "And if the animals ate most of it, there wouldn't be much left for you to find."

"I suppose." She didn't sound convinced. "But I should have still seen something. That stuff spreads quickly, and I find it hard to believe those three animals ate every scrap of the guilty plant."

"Good point," Jose said.

"Wyatt has offered to ride out to the site with me tomorrow." She glanced at him and he nodded, offering silent reassurance he still intended to go with her. "He'll help me search the area for cyanide-producing plants."

Jose smiled at Wyatt. "That's very kind of you."

"My pleasure," Wyatt said.

"Hopefully we'll have more answers tomorrow," Isabel said. "How was your day, Abuelo?"

Jose let out a small sigh. "It was…interesting."

Diego's eyebrows shot up. "Oh?"

The old man gestured to the chair and small sofa nearby. "You should sit. We need to discuss this before dinner. Maria will not like it if we talk business at the table."

Diego claimed the worn chair, leaving the sofa for Isabel and Wyatt. Isabel took a seat, but Wyatt hesitated. "I'll go see if Maria needs any help." He didn't want to intrude on a family meeting.

Jose held up his hand. "No, please stay. I already

know what Diego and Isabel are going to say. It will be good to hear an outside opinion."

"All right." Wyatt slowly lowered himself to sit next to Isabel. The furniture creaked a little under his weight, but neither Diego nor Isabel looked concerned, so he relaxed and leaned back.

"Let me guess." Diego's voice practically dripped with suspicion. "The men from the energy company came back."

"They did," Jose said.

"Did you at least listen to them?" Isabel asked. She sounded exasperated.

"I did," Jose replied.

Diego shifted, leaning forward. Wyatt could tell he was growing agitated. "I can't believe you're actually considering this."

Jose's eyes were full of patience as he focused on his grandson. "It is good to have options."

What was going on here? Wyatt glanced at Isabel for clarification, but she was focused on her grandfather and didn't meet his gaze.

"This is a bad option," Diego muttered.

"Times change," Isabel said. "We should, too."

"Not at the expense of our family legacy!"

"Enough!" Jose's voice cut through the budding argument. Both Diego and Isabel shut their mouths and leaned back, wearing similar expressions of frustration and disgust.

Jose turned to Wyatt. "You've heard of the Praline Energy Corporation?"

Wyatt nodded. It was a local company that had started small and grown rapidly. Now it seemed that any time Wyatt drove into the city of Alpine or one of the other towns near the park he passed several tankers bearing the company's name.

"They're looking to expand their operations. They've gotten into the fracking business, and since they're not allowed to drill within Big Bend, they're trying to get as close to the edges of the park as possible."

"They want to drill here," Wyatt said. Of course they did. The Cruz ranch represented pristine land right on the border of the park. By drilling on the ranch, the company would be obeying the letter of the law, if not quite the spirit.

"Yes," Jose confirmed. "They've made a generous offer for our mineral rights."

"Blood money," Diego said darkly.

Wyatt glanced at him. "I take it you're not a fan?"

"No." He shook his head for emphasis. "The last thing we need is a fracking well on our land. I've heard too many stories of the chemicals and contaminated water leaking into the surrounding area and destroying the land. Not to mention the uptick in the number of earthquakes in the areas where a lot of fracking occurs. It's just not worth it."

"We need the money," Isabel injected. "Expenses are up and profits are down. We have to find some way of increasing revenue if this ranch is going to survive."

"And what if we have a spill, or the release of toxic gas kills our cattle? What if, God forbid, we have an explosion? There won't be a ranch if we let these people on our land to strip away its resources."

"There won't be a ranch if we can't pay our bills," Isabel shot back. "Face it, brother. People don't eat beef like they used to. We've got to adapt."

"Letting the oil company wreck our land for profit is not a viable long-term strategy. Sure, the money would help us out now. But what happens in a few years when they've extracted all they can out of the ground? We'll be stuck with a mess that will take generations to clean up. What good will that do us?"

"It won't be that bad—" Isabel began.

Jose held up his hand, cutting her off. "As you can see," the old man said to Wyatt, "there are several points to consider."

"What do you want to do?" Wyatt asked. He understood why Jose was including Diego and Isabel in the decision-making process; one day the ranch would belong to them. But, ultimately, this was Jose's choice to make.

He shook his head and looked down. "I'm not sure," he confessed. "Isabel is right," he said, glancing up and over to his granddaughter. "We need money. We won't be able to keep going for much longer if we don't figure out a way to increase our profits.

"But," he continued, turning to gaze at Diego, "my grandson makes some good points, as well. If we let this company drill on our land, we run the very real risk of destroying it."

"Do they have to put the well on ranch land?" Wyatt asked. "I know there are some locations where they use horizontal drilling, so the well is located a decent distance away from the shale. Maybe that would work here." He glanced from Diego to Isabel, gauging their acceptance of this possible compromise. "You'd get your funds from the sale of the mineral rights, but the actual drilling would occur off-site, so you don't have to worry about contamination of the land."

"I asked if that was an option," Jose said. "The men from the company said they needed to put the well here to maximize its output."

"In other words," Diego said, temper flaring in his brown eyes, "they're quite happy to have us assume all the risk of property damage in case something goes wrong."

"It sounds like there's no good compromise to be found," Wyatt said.

"There isn't," Isabel agreed. "We either take a chance on a better future, or keep our heads in the mud and hope things will go back to the way they were."

"I'm not in denial about our situation," Diego snapped. "I'm just not willing to wreck our environment for a little financial gain."

Isabel shot to her feet and began to pace the confines of the office. "Why won't you wake up and see what's in front of you?" She tucked a stray strand of hair behind her ear with one hand and gestured with the other. "Praline Energy is not going to go away. They want our natural gas, and they're going to find a way to take it. Right now, they're trying to play nice by making us a generous offer. If we refuse, they'll try another approach."

"They can't just take our property," Diego said.

"Maybe not outright," Isabel shot back. "But they'll get the state to declare eminent domain like they did for the pipeline a few years ago. Make no mistake—these guys are not going to accept no for an answer."

"So you think we should just roll over without a fight?" Diego stood, gesturing out the window to the land beyond. "We should just sign away our ranch with a smile and say thank you for not taking it by force?"

"Of course not! But if we cooperate with them, we might be able to shape the terms of the deal. I'd rather have a bit of control over the situation, wouldn't you?"

"We do have control," Diego insisted. "This is our ranch. Our land. Our decision." There was no mistaking the passion in his voice.

"I'd like to hear what Wyatt thinks about all of this." Jose's voice was quiet, but as soon as he spoke, his grandchildren went silent. Three heads swiveled in his direction, three pairs of brown eyes focused on him.

Wyatt swallowed, trying to tamp down a surge of anxiety. He cared about these people, and in the case of Jose and Diego, thought of them as family. No matter what he said, someone he loved was going to be disappointed in him.

"I understand the ranch needs to bring in money," he said. He met Isabel's eyes, knowing his next words were going to hurt her. "But I don't think fracking is the way to do it."

Diego smiled in triumph. Isabel merely shook her head, her disappointment obvious.

"Come on, guys," Wyatt said pleadingly. "I'm a park ranger. You know how I feel about the environment. I get where you're coming from, and I understand what you're saying about trying to control the situation. But there are ways we can fight back so they won't over-rule your refusal to let them drill."

Isabel's eyes flicked from Wyatt to Diego, suspicion building along with her temper. He could tell from the look on her face she thought he was only siding with her brother because of their friendship. "We, Wyatt? There is no 'we' here. This is Cruz Ranch business. Last time I checked, you're not one of us."

The hit landed, but Wyatt refused to flinch. *I deserved that.*

"Isabel." Jose's tone was censorious. "That is no way to treat a friend."

A flicker of regret passed over Isabel's face but she remained silent.

"It's all right," Wyatt said. He ran a hand through his hair, hating that he'd contributed to this rift in the family. "She's right. I shouldn't get involved." He stood, tilted his head toward Jose. "Thanks for your hospitality. I think I should probably collect my horse and head out. I don't want to upset anyone by staying." A lump formed in his stomach as he realized he'd just destroyed the tentative truce they'd reached in Diego's room.

Everyone spoke at the same time.

"No."

"Absolutely not."

Wyatt glanced at Isabel, surprised by her response. She shook her head. "You don't need to leave. You're our guest. And our friend," she added. "We're not going to have you set off by yourself at night. It's not safe."

Her words were an echo of what he'd said to her ten years ago. A tingle shot down his spine at the memory.

Isabel must have felt something, too. Her eyes widened briefly and she glanced away.

"Please stay," said Jose. "This argument has been going on for weeks. It's not going to be resolved tonight. I value your input." He glanced at his grandchildren. "And your honesty."

Maria appeared in the doorway. She read the room in a glance and nodded to herself. "Come. It's time to eat. Leave your discussion in this room. There will be no fighting at my table."

Diego helped his grandfather stand and the pair of them headed for the door. Wyatt hung back, hoping to have a word with Isabel.

"I'm sorry," he said when they were alone. "I know my answer upset you."

"It's fine." Isabel brushed aside the apology. "I wasn't surprised. I know what you do for a living."

"No hard feelings?"

Isabel shook her head. "Just tell me this. If Diego had thought drilling was a good idea, and I'd been the one to argue against it, would your answer still be the same?"

Wyatt's stomach flip-flopped. "Of course. Why do you ask?"

"Because I know your friendship runs deep," Isabel said. "I already feel like the deck is stacked against me—Diego doesn't want to listen to my thoughts on the matter. But we have to do something or the ranch won't last. I'm not exactly celebrating the idea of letting the oil company drill on our land. It's simply the best offer we have right now, and I think we should take it while we can."

"Surely there's another way?" Wyatt suggested. "A compromise you can all agree on?"

Isabel shook her head. "I haven't found one yet."

"You will." He was confident a solution would present itself. "You're the smartest person I know, Isabel. You'll come up with something."

"Maybe," she murmured. "I wish it were that simple."

"I'll do some brainstorming, too," he offered. "We can work on the issue together." Once again, he was inserting himself into her family's affairs. But he couldn't stand to see her looking so frustrated and worried. Maybe the two of them could come up with an idea that would bring in money for the ranch so they wouldn't have to accept the energy company's offer.

Isabel's eyes widened a bit. "You really want to do that?"

"Yeah," he replied. "I do." The Cruz family was his family. Anything that helped them out made him feel good. But his motives weren't entirely altruistic; he knew his suggestion meant he'd be spending more time with Isabel.

After their near kiss in Diego's bedroom, it was a sacrifice he was all too happy to make.

Chapter 5

Isabel sat in the breakfast nook of the kitchen, clutching her coffee cup the way a drowning man might grip a life preserver. She was no stranger to sleepless nights—in her training to become a vet, she'd worked countless hours and dealt with the fragmented sleep that accompanied call shifts at a busy animal hospital. But last night had been different. Her emotions had been all over the map thanks to their pre-dinner family argument, the increasing stress of the energy company's attention and the three dead cattle.

Oh, and the man who'd dropped back into her life.

Her knee-jerk desire to avoid Wyatt was fading. That old familiar tug of attraction was taking its place. There was just something about the man that pulled her, made her want to get closer. She'd thought the passage of time would have changed things, made her less susceptible to his presence. But, if anything, she found herself even more drawn to him, as though she needed to make up for lost time.

Even the fact that he'd taken her brother's side in last night's argument hadn't been enough to shake off the hold he still had over her. She knew he didn't support the plan to drill on the land, and she understood why he wouldn't. As a park ranger, he was all about conservation and protecting the environment. Those were admirable traits, and Isabel didn't necessarily disagree with his stance.

But the ranch's accounting books painted a grim picture of the future of the business. And as much as she might want to sit around a campfire and sing about the circle of life, that attitude wasn't going to pay the bills.

He'd surprised her with his offer to help brainstorm a solution to their money problems. Maybe they'd actually come up with something. But she feared this gesture was merely his attempt to bridge this ideological rift between them. It was a nice thought, but was there any common ground between her pragmatism and his starry-eyed idealism?

It doesn't matter, she told herself. She and Wyatt didn't have to come to a compromise because they weren't emotionally involved. He was Diego's friend, and the two of them didn't need to share the same outlook to be polite to each other when they were all together.

She'd just have to go back to lusting after his body from afar. A tingle started in her stomach as she pictured his bare chest, his skin still damp from the shower. She hadn't meant to watch him dress last night, but she hadn't been able to take her eyes off that expanse of lean muscle and golden skin, or the inverted triangle of dark hair that tapered into a straight line, bisecting his belly and dipping below the waistband of his pants…

She took another sip of coffee and sighed, closing her eyes as the caffeine began to take hold. She heard the scrape of ceramic on the table and opened her eyes to find Maria had slid a plate of food in front of her.

"Gracias," she murmured, grateful for both the food and the distraction.

Maria eyed her from her position at the stove. "You didn't sleep." It wasn't a question.

Isabel set down her coffee cup and picked up a tortilla. "I'm fine." She placed a piece of bacon on the tortilla, then piled eggs on the strip.

"You're not." Maria brought over a bowl of shredded cheese and a container of salsa. "You need to rest. It's not good for you to work the way you do."

Isabel smiled and patted the empty spot at the table next to her. Maria sat, watching her as Isabel added cheese and salsa to her burrito. Once all the ingredients were in place, Isabel folded the tortilla and offered it to Maria.

The older woman shook her head. "Mami," Isabel said softly, "you're a fine one to talk about working too hard."

Maria narrowed her eyes but took the proffered food. "That's different," she said, taking a bite. "It's my job to take care of you all."

"And it's my job to see to the animals," Isabel said, knowing it was futile to dispute Maria's statement. They were all adults, but Maria had the soul of a caregiver. Isabel knew the other woman was happiest when she had someone to look after. Still, she and Diego tried to make things easy for her.

"Things will slow down after calving season ends," Isabel continued. "You know how it is."

"*Sí*. And I also know I have never seen you and your brother so at odds before."

Isabel folded her own burrito and took a bite. "That will be fine, too," she said.

Maria's eyes were kind. "One of you will be very disappointed by your *abuelo*'s decision. You will both have to come together to live with the consequences."

Isabel's mouth went dry. She swallowed, washing the food down with another sip of coffee. "I know," she said softly. "I hope it won't take too long."

"It won't." Maria sounded more confident than Isabel felt. "Your brother is a good man. He can be overbearing, but his heart is in the right place. You two will work through this."

"Have you seen him this morning?" Diego had been uncharacteristically quiet during last night's dinner, and had gone to his room soon after the meal was over.

Maria shook her head. "I heard him leave this morning. He hasn't come back for breakfast yet."

"Maybe he's avoiding me," Isabel murmured.

"Perhaps," Maria agreed. "But if you wait long enough, his stomach will get the better of his pride."

Isabel smiled. "You're right, but I don't have that kind of time. I have my own things to do today."

The clomp of footsteps on the stairs announced Wyatt's arrival before he even stepped into the kitchen. He paused in the doorway. "Good morning, ladies."

"Come in, come in." Maria beckoned him forward with a wave. She stood and walked to the coffeepot. "You sit. I'll get you some breakfast."

A startled look crossed Wyatt's face, as if he hadn't been expecting such a warm welcome. He sat in Maria's vacated chair. "Thank you, Tía."

She tsked as she brought him a cup of coffee. "I hope you like it black," Isabel said softly. "Maria is philosophically opposed to cream, and she thinks sugar should only be used for baking."

A smile played at the corners of Wyatt's mouth. "This is fine," he murmured. "It's hot, which is all

I care about." He took a sip, watching her over the rim of the mug. "Long night?"

"How'd you know?"

His gaze tracked over her face, lingering on the dark circles under her eyes. "Just a hunch," he replied.

Maria slid a plate of food in front of him. He smiled up at her, his blue eyes glowing with genuine affection. His expression made Isabel's breath hitch. He was so handsome—like a cowboy out of central casting rather than a real person.

He glanced over, caught her watching him. His mouth curved in a half smile, the question plain. Isabel shook her head and looked down, focusing on her breakfast.

They ate in companionable silence, the faint sounds of birdsong drifting in through the partially open window. Isabel could feel the weight of Maria's gaze as the older woman studied the two of them, clearly speculating as to the nature of things. There would be questions later, of that Isabel was certain. But at least Maria seemed content to wait to ask them until they were alone again.

Wyatt cleaned his plate quickly. Isabel tilted her head back for the last sip of coffee and then set the cup on the table.

"Are you still willing to go back to the site with me?" Maybe he'd changed his mind last night. After witnessing the argument between her and Diego and finding out she supported drilling on the land, Isabel wouldn't really blame Wyatt if he wanted to put some distance between him and her family.

"Absolutely." He pushed his chair back, got to his feet and grabbed both his empty plate and her own.

Maria intercepted him before he made it to the sink. "Go." She shooed them both out of the kitchen.

Wyatt leaned down to give the older woman a hug. "Thank you for your hospitality. I hope I get to see you again soon."

Maria wrapped her arms around his waist, the top of her head coming to the level of his sternum. "You are always welcome here. And I think you'll return sooner than you expect." Still folded in Wyatt's embrace, she turned her head to look at Isabel. Her expression was knowing, as though she'd already seen the future.

Isabel glanced away, her cheeks growing hot.

"I hope you're right." From the corner of her eye, Isabel saw Wyatt release Maria with a smile. "Until then, take care."

"You, too, *mijo*," Maria replied. She reached up with one hand to gently pat his cheek.

Isabel's heart warmed at the sight. There was such love between the two of them; there always had been. It was just another element of Wyatt's personality. Women of all ages seemed drawn to him.

Wyatt turned to Isabel. "Ready?"

She nodded. "Let's saddle up."

It was a short walk to the barn and, as they were both experienced riders, it didn't take them long to get everything in place for the ride. Both Miel and Wyatt's horse, Ajax, seemed happy to head out into the sunshine. Isabel closed her eyes as the warmth spread across her shoulders, relaxing muscles she hadn't realized were tense.

"Beautiful day," Wyatt observed.

She inhaled deeply, enjoying the green scent of grass, the rich, earthy tang of fresh manure and the sharp twinge of sage. It was a perfume unlike any other, the aroma unique to the ranch. "Yes, it is."

They stuck to a walking pace—no need to rush on this pretty morning. The wind tugged at her hat, but the random gusts weren't strong enough to knock it off her head. Isabel was surprised at how much she was enjoying herself. Maybe it was the lack of sleep last night, or perhaps it was the look Maria had given her in the kitchen; either way, Isabel decided to take advantage of their solitude.

"How's your grandfather?" Wyatt's parents had abandoned him when he was young, and he'd been raised by his grandfather. Isabel had met him a couple of times when Maria had insisted the older man join them for a meal. He'd been a quiet but pleasant man, unfailingly polite. She hoped he was still alive—she hated the thought of Wyatt being without any family.

"He's fine," Wyatt said. "He moves a lot slower these days, but his spirits are still high. I try to visit at least once a week."

"I'm sure he appreciates that."

"It's good for both of us." He gave her a smile that made her heart melt a little. "Now it's my turn for a question. How long have you been back?"

"A few months. I finished my internship in large animal medicine and came back here."

"I was surprised to see you yesterday. I thought you wanted to open your own practice in Houston."

"I did," she admitted. "But the more time I spent away from the ranch, the more I realized how much I missed it. Growing up here, I couldn't wait to get away. But once I did, I realized how special this place is."

"I hear that," Wyatt said. "I did some of my training in Arizona. Several of my classmates were surprised that I wanted to work in Big Bend."

"Oh? Is it an unpopular choice?"

"It's no Yellowstone or Grand Canyon," Wyatt said. "Big Bend is one of the most overlooked parks, from a visitation perspective. Life moves a bit slower out here as a consequence." He shrugged. "Not everyone likes that."

"But you do."

He was quiet a moment, considering her words. "My life is here. It has been since I was a kid. There's something to be said for having friends and family nearby."

She nodded. "That's what called me home, too. Now it's hard to imagine why I wanted to be elsewhere."

"You have a support system here. Family is everything."

She looked at him. He seemed to want to say more and, before she knew it, she blurted out, "Do you ever think about starting your own family?" It was a question that weighed heavily on her own mind at times. She loved her brother and Maria and Abuelo. She loved the ranch. But Wyatt was right—not everyone was cut out for this kind of life.

If she'd stayed in a city, set up her own practice there, it would have been much easier to find someone. Out here with the nearest town over fifty miles away? It was a little harder. There wasn't exactly a glut of men her age who were interested in a relationship. Sometimes Isabel lay awake at night, wondering if she'd made a mistake by coming back. She wanted to help preserve the family ranch, but what if she was so wrapped up in the present she neglected her own future?

"Yeah." The word came out on a sigh. "I do. But it's not easy to meet people out here."

"You've noticed that, too?" she teased.

He smiled. "You've only been back a few months. Already getting twitchy?"

Isabel shrugged. "Just thinking about the future."

"I get it. I'm kicking around a few ideas myself."

"Like what?" She was curious to hear what he was thinking. As best as she could tell, most of the people she and Diego had gone to school with had left the area. They seemed to be the lone holdouts.

"Well…once my grandfather is gone, I might put in for a transfer. Try to move to a spot that's closer to a city. I figure that would make it easier to have more of a personal life."

The thought of Wyatt having a relationship with anyone triggered a flare of green fire in her chest. Isabel quickly quashed the spurt of jealousy—she had no claim over him. Never had. And there was certainly no connection between them now.

Still, the thought of him leaving the area was upsetting. Wyatt had always been a part of the collage of people and places that she considered "home." The realization that he might not always be around created a small cold spot in her heart.

She was saved from having to reply by their arrival at the spot of yesterday's discovery. "Let's leave the horses over there." She pointed to a large bush several yards away. "If there are any toxic plants in the area, I don't want them exposed."

"Good plan," Wyatt said. They dismounted, leaving Ajax and Miel to keep each other company as they walked back to the slope where she'd found the cattle.

Isabel stood at the rim of the shallow depression, scanning the ground. The red dirt still bore the marks of yesterday's activity. A few plants grew in scraggly clumps nearby, but nothing like the density that would be needed to take down three large animals.

She glanced over and saw Wyatt frowning. "See anything?"

He shook his head. "Not really. There is some Johnson grass here—" he pointed to one spot, then another "—but wouldn't it take a large dose of cyanide to kill three cattle?"

"Yes," she confirmed. "They're used to consuming a certain amount as a normal part of grazing. For three animals to drop dead like that means they ingested a large amount of the toxin in a short period of time." She looked around, eyeing the small bushes that dotted the ground. "Are any of those toxic?"

Wyatt followed her gaze. "No."

"Well, they had to pick up the poison from somewhere." Isabel started walking, scanning the ground as she moved in a widening circle around the incline. "Cyanide doesn't just appear from thin air."

"True," Wyatt said. "I hate to be a downer, but I don't see anything out here that would be toxic to cattle."

Isabel opened her mouth to respond but a scattering of hay in the dirt caught her eye. That was odd—they didn't drop hay bales this close to the border fence with the park, as they didn't want to draw deer and other grazers onto the ranch. Why was there a collection of it here?

She followed the bits of hay for several yards until she came to a spot that boasted a small pile of the golden strands. "Where did this come from?"

A dull metal object was in the center of the mound. "What the hell?" she muttered. She knelt to study it further.

"Find something?" Wyatt called.

"Maybe," she replied. She brushed some of the hay aside to find a metal stake buried in the ground with a few inches of hollow tube exposed. She'd never seen anything like it before, and it definitely didn't belong there. She reached out to clear more of the dirt and hay away with one hand, wanting to expose the rest of this strange device.

Wyatt's boots made a crunching sound in the grass as he walked over. "Whatcha got?"

"Some kind of weird metal tube," she said, brushing at the dirt.

"What?" He approached from the opposite side, casting the tube in shadow as he loomed overhead. "Get back!"

Isabel froze, the note of alarm in his voice making her heart thump hard. She glanced up to find him staring down at her in shock, his face unnaturally pale. He reached out with his hand, clearly trying to ward her away from her discovery. "Isabel, I'm serious. Get away from that. Right now."

Alarmed by his reaction, she leaned back on her heels and put a hand on the ground for balance. But just as she began to rise, a gust of wind sent a spray of hay and dirt into her face.

Between one breath and the next, Isabel's eyes felt like they'd caught fire. She gasped in pain, instinctively reaching up to rub her eyes. Her mouth flooded with saliva, choking her. Tears streamed down her cheeks but brought no relief to the burning tissue.

She rocked forward onto her knees, spitting into the dirt so she could breathe.

Her heart thundered in her ears, but she heard Wyatt's voice over the din. He cursed loudly then yelled her name. Isabel squinted up through swollen lids, her vision blurry as she tried to find him. But she couldn't see him, couldn't even speak thanks to a new rush of saliva filling her mouth.

A tight band wrapped around her chest, making it hard to breathe. She felt the wind on her face and realized she was moving, but little else. Her senses were haywire and everything seemed to be happening far away.

"Hold on," Wyatt yelled into her ear. "We're almost there."

She landed hard on her bottom. A split second later, a flood of cold water poured over her face, making her gasp and sputter even more. Had he emptied his canteen on her? What was happening?

"Open your eyes," Wyatt commanded.

Isabel tried, but the lids wouldn't part very far.

Wyatt used his fingers to pry them open and then flushed them with more water. The cool liquid brought some measure of relief, but the water flooding into her nose and mouth made her feel like she was drowning.

She tried to speak, the words scraping her throat like razor blades. "What was that?"

"An M44 trap." He spoke quickly, his tone urgent. His hands fumbled at her belt, unclipping her walkie-talkie. "Diego, come in."

She heard a burst of static then her brother's voice. "Wyatt? Is that you?"

"We've had an accident. Call 9-1-1. Tell them we have a case of cyanide poisoning and we need a helicopter right away."

"What happened?"

Isabel struggled to breathe as Wyatt helped her to stand. Fear licked down her spine even as her clinician's mind clicked into gear. Cyanide. The poison kept her body from using oxygen—no wonder she was so desperate for air.

"There's no time," he said. "We're headed back to the ranch house. Have the helicopter land nearby."

She didn't hear her brother's reply. Her head was pounding, the pain all-encompassing.

"Okay, I need you to help me out." It took her a second to realize Wyatt was talking to her. She reached out blindly, made contact with the fabric of his shirt. Gripping it tightly, she had to turn her head and spit again.

Wyatt wrapped a large hand around her wrist. The contact steadied her, made her feel less alone. "Let's get you on your horse."

There was no way she could ride by herself. "I can't—" Her throat closed up, trapping the words. She coughed, but it didn't help.

"I know," he said, correctly interpreting her protest. "Just trust me."

He released her wrist, shifted away for a second. Something large moved in front of her and Wyatt placed her hands on Miel's saddle. "Grip here," he said. "As tight as you can."

She tried to cooperate, but she was so focused on drawing air into her lungs it was hard to do anything else. Wyatt boosted her up into the saddle. Her stomach roiled at the sudden change in position. "Hang on. Just for a second."

She heard the creak of leather nearby. Then she felt Wyatt's hands on her again, pulling her off her horse and onto his own. She was helpless, still unable to open her eyes beyond slits, her mind trapped by the throbbing in her head and the constant struggle for breath. "There you go," he said calmly, settling her in front of him. "We need to make time, so hold on as best as you can."

Before she could try to reply, he wrapped one arm around her waist and kicked his mount into a gallop. Overwhelmed by pain, frightened out of her mind, Isabel could do little more than bounce along like a sack of potatoes.

"You're going to be okay." Wyatt yelled to be heard over the rush of wind and the sound of the horse's hooves striking the ground. His arm tightened around her, his body cradling her from behind as he rushed her home. "Don't worry—it's going to be fine." He was trying to be strong for her. But no amount of false bravado could mask the fear in his voice.

Isabel wanted to believe him. But she couldn't stop thinking about those three cattle, lying dead in the dirt. How long had it taken them to succumb?

And how much time did she have until she shared their fate?

Wyatt paced the hallway outside Isabel's hospital room, hoping the constant movement would help burn off the adrenaline that was still pulsing through his body.

How had this happened? One minute, he and Isabel had been looking for suspicious plants. The next thing he knew, he was galloping back to the ranch house with Isabel in his arms, her body growing increasingly limp against his chest.

They'd made it back in record time thanks to Ajax's sure-footedness. Diego had beaten them to the house, and was standing outside waiting for them. He'd helped Wyatt get Isabel to the ground, peppering him with a million and one questions that Wyatt couldn't answer.

Fortunately, the medevac had arrived quickly.

Wyatt ran a hand through his hair, dislodging some of the dirt and grit the rotor wash had kicked into the air as the chopper had landed. He'd tried to step back so Diego could ride with Isabel to the hospital, but she'd refused to release his hand. So he'd climbed in after her, finding a seat by her feet and trying his best to stay out of the way as the medics attended to her.

They hadn't asked too many questions. He'd told them about the cyanide trap and they'd quickly started an IV line in her arm, adding some bright red liquid to the bag of saline. Within a few minutes, Isabel's body had started to relax, her breathing falling into a more normal pattern. By the time they landed at the medical center in Alpine, some ninety miles away, she was no longer gasping for air.

Wyatt hadn't had any time alone with her since they'd arrived at the hospital. As soon as the helicopter's landing gear had touched the roof, a team of people in scrubs had rushed over and pulled Isabel's gurney free from the body of the chopper. They'd set off for the door at a run and Wyatt had barely been able to keep up as they'd whisked her to the emergency room.

Things were a little calmer now. Once the medical team had determined she was stable, she'd been transferred to a room. A nurse was in there now, checking her vital signs to make sure she didn't have a setback.

Diego, Jose and Maria were all on their way. Wyatt had called with updates on Isabel's condition, wanting them to know she was recovering. He knew they were still panicked, of course. Truth be told, so was he. Seeing her with his own eyes didn't alleviate all his worry.

His mind kept going back to the last moment she'd been okay, before the wind had picked up and carried the poison right into her face. Seeing her kneeling in the dirt, inches away from that deadly trap, had taken years off his life. Even now, his stomach heaved at the memory.

Where had it come from? M44 traps were generally used to control coyote or feral dog populations. They were designed to deliver a blast of cyanide into the mouth of an animal that tugged on the attached bait. They were effective but not selective, as many dog owners had discovered over the years. In recent months, public outcry had grown to the point the USDA was considering no longer using the traps.

To Wyatt's knowledge, no such devices had been deployed in Big Bend National Park. And since Isabel hadn't immediately recognized it for what it was, he was willing to bet the Cruz Ranch didn't use them, either.

He closed his eyes, envisioning the scene. There had been a scattering of hay on the ground, a larger pile of it on the trap that she'd been trying to clear away.

Bait, he realized.

His blood turned to ice as the implications set in. This was no accident, no trap set years ago and then forgotten about as time passed. Someone had trespassed on ranch land, deliberately placed the trap and then baited it to draw cattle.

Sabotage.

Was it connected to the destruction of the fence panel? Or was it simply an unfortunate coincidence? It was hard to know how long the spike had been in the ground, though the hay used to bait the trap had seemed fairly fresh.

Wyatt's mind kept churning as he walked. Who had done this? More importantly, were there other traps out there, waiting to deliver their deadly cargo to the unsuspecting animals or people who stumbled over them?

The hinges on the hospital room door squeaked softly as it was opened. Wyatt turned in time to see the nurse walk out. She paused when she caught sight of him standing there, her eyebrows coming together in a frown.

"Are you all right?"

"Yeah," he replied automatically. He took a deep breath, trying to smooth his expression so his shock and worry wasn't so obvious. "I'm fine. How's she doing?"

"Holding steady. You can go in if you want. She asked for you."

Pleasure bloomed in his chest, followed closely by a wave of relief. If Isabel was asking for him, she must be feeling better.

He knocked softly on the door to her room then pushed it open and walked inside.

Isabel was reclining in the bed, her hair dark against the white pillow. Wyatt studied her as he moved closer. She was frighteningly pale, her skin almost the same shade as the hospital gown she wore. A tube, draped over her ears and across her cheekbones, rested just under her nose. More tubes, attached to her arm, had ends connected to a box on a pole that emitted a whirring sound. She seemed small and so, so fragile.

"Hey." Her voice was a rasp that had him wincing in sympathy.

"Hey yourself." He stopped by the side of her bed. Without thinking, he reached for her hand. He needed to touch her, to know she was still there and would eventually be okay again.

She squeezed his hand, her brown eyes warm as she stared up at him. "You saved my life."

The image of the dead cattle flashed in Wyatt's mind. *That could have been you*, he realized, horror making his knees weak. What if she'd gone back to the site alone, discovered the trap with no one around to help her? She'd be lying in the dirt now, with no one the wiser until it was too late.

He sank onto the chair near the bed. "I'm just glad you're okay." The words came out a little shaky, a reflection of his inner turmoil.

"Thanks to you. What was that thing? Did you recognize it, or did you just have a hunch it was dangerous?"

"It's a cyanide trap." He explained its use and the mechanism by which it worked. "The Department of Agriculture has a history of using them."

She frowned. "Do you think someone from the park put one there?"

Wyatt shook his head. "As far as I know, we don't use them in Big Bend. Besides, your property is clearly fenced in that area. Anyone setting traps for a legitimate reason wouldn't dream of trespassing."

"So this was deliberate."

"Yes." He nodded for emphasis. "Your family is on the way. I think you all should seriously consider calling the sheriff's department." If it were up to him, he would have called them already. But he wasn't sure how Isabel would want to handle the situation. And it was entirely possible the sheriff wouldn't be able to do anything—there were no surveillance cameras along the fence, no way to identify who had set the trap or when. They might not ever discover who had done this, but it would make Wyatt feel better to report it.

"Hand me the phone." She gestured to the slim receiver on the bedside table. "I'm not going to wait for Abuelo or Diego to give me permission. We lost three cattle, and I would have died if you hadn't been there. That's got to be attempted murder, at the least."

Wyatt passed her the phone, glad to hear she agreed with his unspoken opinion. "Let me find the number for you." He pulled out his cell phone for a quick internet search.

"What happened to Miel?" Isabel sounded worried. "I was so focused on breathing I forgot about her. Did you leave her out there by the trap?"

"No." Ignoring the phone for a moment, he focused on her again. She was leaning forward, her eyes wide as her teeth worried at her bottom lip.

"She's okay," he continued. He smiled, trying to

reassure her. "She chased after Ajax when we set off for the house. Guess she didn't want to be left alone out there. Ruben took care of both her and Ajax once we got back."

Isabel relaxed back onto the pillow. "That's good," she said, relief evident in her tone. "Now we just have to keep the other animals away from the spot."

"Ruben's taking care of that, too. He was there when I told your brother what had happened. Said he'd ride out to the spot and put up a makeshift fence to keep the rest of the herd away from the trap."

"What would we do without Ruben?" Isabel asked softly.

"Let's hope your family never has to find out," Wyatt said. "Ready for the sheriff's number?"

Isabel nodded, dialing as he recited the digits. A few minutes later, after making a report to the authorities, she replaced the phone in its cradle and handed it back to him.

"Well?" he asked.

"A couple of deputies are going to come to the hospital to speak to me," she said. "They'll also go to the ranch to check things out there."

"Good," Wyatt replied. He wasn't sure how much they'd actually discover, but maybe they'd get lucky.

"Do you…" She trailed off, a contemplative look on her face. He stayed quiet, waiting for her to finish her thought. A second later, she shook her head in silent dismissal.

"Do you think there are more traps?" she asked, meeting his eyes once more.

"I think we have to assume so. Or at least act as if there are. Diego is going to need to scout that area with a fine-toothed comb to make sure there aren't any lurking."

"I bet there are," she murmured. "Whoever cut the fence was probably the same person to set the trap. And I doubt they stopped at just one."

"Probably not," Wyatt agreed. "So your workers should employ the buddy system when they're out checking fences or looking for signs of calving."

"Good idea." She was quiet a moment, but he could tell from the look in her eyes her mind was engaged. "Do you think the energy company had anything to do with this?"

Wyatt considered the possibility. "I doubt it," he said. "I can't imagine they'd sanction the illegal placement of cyanide traps on your land. That opens them up to a big lawsuit."

"Only if we can prove it was them," Isabel pointed out. "Given the remoteness of the area, we'd practically have to catch them in the act to prove they're involved."

"That's true," Wyatt said. "What makes you think they're part of this?"

She lifted one shoulder in a shrug. "I'm just guessing at this point." She rested her head against the pillow, closing her eyes. It was clear she was exhausted, and no wonder. Her body had spent a good deal of time fighting to breathe this morning. After that kind of traumatic experience, rest was the best thing for her.

"Let's worry about it later," Wyatt suggested. He understood her desire to get to the bottom of this mystery, but she needed to recover. She wasn't the type to willingly take a break. Hopefully her doctors would force the issue, since she was unlikely to listen to him or to her family on this matter.

Isabel opened her eyes. "Are you suggesting I let it go? Because I can promise you, that's not going to happen."

Wyatt held up a hand in defense. "Not at all. I just think you've had one hell of a morning. It wouldn't be a bad thing if you rested for a bit. No one is going to forget about today's events." *Especially not me,* he added silently, feeling a tremor run through him again at the memory of her kneeling inches away from the trap. "But there's nothing you can do from your hospital bed to fix things. The deputies and your family are on their way. Talk to them, let them do some of the work. Give yourself time to heal. Then you can dive back in and take on the world."

A ghost of a smile flitted across her face. "Why do you have to sound so reasonable?"

He tilted his head to the side. "I'm sorry?" he said with a smile.

She laughed, the sound quickly turning into a cough that made her wince. Her face turned red as the spasm gripped her.

Alarmed, Wyatt leaned forward. He wanted to help, but what could he do besides offer moral support?

There was a large plastic glass on the bedside table. He grabbed it and rushed to the sink on the far wall, quickly filling it with water. She reached for it as he turned around, but it was several seconds before she dared to take a drink.

"Thanks," she said finally. Her voice was like sandpaper on his ears. She opened her mouth to speak again, but Wyatt shook his head.

"Please, don't push yourself." *I can't watch you do that anymore.*

She nodded, leaned back against the pillow again.

Wyatt watched her for a moment, the tension leaving his body as she relaxed once more. Her chest rose and fell in a steady, normal rhythm, something he didn't think he'd take for granted ever again.

Assuming she was asleep, he took a step toward the door. Maybe he could catch Diego and the rest of the family in the hall, keep them from running into the room and waking her up. But before he could take another step, Isabel spoke.

"Please stay."

Wyatt turned around. Her eyes were still closed but she'd moved her head to face the door. When he didn't respond right away, she opened her eyes. "I don't want to be alone right now."

Her confession was like an arrow to his heart. Isabel was a strong, independent woman with a healthy dose of pride. Growing up, she'd never asked for help, even if she'd clearly needed it. For her to say this now meant she had to be feeling incredibly vulnerable.

"Of course," he said softly. He returned to her side, settling into the chair once more. "I won't leave you."

Isabel smiled, her eyes closing again. Wyatt sat in silence, watching as she sank into sleep. His heart flip-flopped at the sight, and the emotions he'd pushed aside earlier while in crisis mode rose to the surface and began demanding his attention.

Twenty-four hours. That's all it had taken for Isabel to reclaim her spot in his life. He still didn't know why she'd left without saying goodbye all those years ago, or what he'd done to cause the rift between them. But those worries paled in significance compared to the events of this morning.

She could have died in his arms. Probably would have, if the medevac hadn't arrived when it had. And even though they hadn't spoken to each other in ten years, the thought of a world without Isabel in it was enough to make his blood run cold.

With the adrenaline still fading from his system, Wyatt recognized he wasn't in a good frame of mind to be making decisions. But there were a few things he did know for certain.

He wanted Isabel in his life again.

He needed to find out what had happened between them.

And he'd stay until she asked him to go.

Chapter 6

"What the hell were you thinking?" Diego braced his hands on the metal frame at the foot of Isabel's bed and leaned forward, looming over her ankles.

"Language!" Maria admonished.

Diego flicked a glance in her direction. "Sorry, Mami," he murmured. Then his brown eyes cut back to Isabel, the accusation plain. "What made you think it was a good idea to get so close to a cyanide trap?"

Isabel took a careful breath, hoping to avoid triggering another coughing spasm. Her head still ached, but at least the nausea had faded. *It's the little things*, she thought to herself.

She glanced at her *abuelo*, sitting off to the side of her bed in the room's only chair. He was watching her closely, as if he thought she might start choking at any moment. The lines of his face seemed deeper somehow, his usual vigor dimmed in the artificial lights of the room.

Maria, unable to stand still, puttered around the room shaking out and refolding spare blankets and refreshing Isabel's water. Her concern manifested as action, her worry driving her to move, to do something she considered helpful.

Isabel could handle her grandfather's silence. She appreciated Maria's attempts to comfort her. But she wasn't sure how much of Diego's temper she could tolerate right now.

Where is Wyatt? she thought, irritated.

He'd stepped into the hall when her family had arrived, muttering something about privacy. It was a nice gesture, but she needed him there, running interference with her brother. She stared longingly at the door, wondering if she could pull him back into the room through sheer force of will.

"Well?" Diego demanded.

Isabel glanced at him, noted the fear in his brown eyes. He did love her, even if he had an annoying way of showing it.

"I didn't realize it was a cyanide trap," she explained. Talking made her throat ache, but she couldn't avoid it. The sheriff's deputies would be here soon and she'd have to tell them her story, as well.

"Do you really think I'd deliberately be that reckless?" she continued. Her temper was flaring in response to Diego's accusation. He'd always used his position as older brother to treat her like a child. She was beyond tired of his attitude.

He pushed off the bed rail, ran a hand through his hair. "No," he muttered. "I don't think you did it on purpose. But you still should have known better."

Isabel rolled her eyes. "Sure. Whatever you say." Just how she was supposed to have recognized a trap she'd never seen before remained a mystery, but she didn't have the energy to argue the point right now.

She turned to her grandfather, still sitting quietly. "Is there any chance the trap is one of ours? I know we don't use them now, but maybe they were deployed in the past?"

Jose started shaking his head before she'd even finished the question. "No. We've never used them. Too risky."

"Then where did this one come from?" Diego started to pace, forcing Maria to dodge him as he walked the width of the hospital room. "Who would plant this trap on our land?"

"Probably the same person who cut the fence," Isabel remarked.

Diego nodded, his brows drawn together in a frown. "The last time someone checked the fence was three days ago. It was still intact at that point."

"So sometime in the last three days, the fence was cut and the trap set." Isabel rubbed her forehead with her fingers, trying to ease the persistent ache.

"You are in pain?" Maria asked. She patted Isabel's knee. "I will tell the nurse." She walked away without waiting for a response. Isabel considered telling her not to bother, but she knew it would make the older woman happy if she felt like she had something to do.

"That tells us the when," Diego said. "But we still don't know who or why."

Her brother's musings were interrupted by a knock on the door. A man stepped inside, wearing the khaki shirt and gold star of a sheriff's deputy. "Isabel Cruz?"

"That's me."

He nodded, walked forward until he stood by the side of her bed. "I'm Deputy Jackson. I'm here to talk to you about what happened this morning."

The deputy was a couple of inches shorter than Diego, but he was built like a linebacker with broad shoulders and muscular arms. His gray eyes betrayed no emotion as he glanced at her grandfather and brother, nodding a greeting to both men.

"All right." Isabel pushed up in the bed, wanting to sit forward rather than recline for this interview. "Should we have Wyatt come in? He was with me when everything happened."

"My partner is speaking to him now, ma'am," Deputy Jackson said. "We caught him in the hallway."

"Should we leave?" Jose asked. He placed his hands on the armrests of the chair and began to rise.

Both Deputy Jackson and Diego moved to help

the older man, but Jose waved them off. "I'm fine," he announced. "Just a little creaky."

"There's no need for you to go," the deputy said. "Unless Ms. Cruz would prefer to speak to me alone."

Isabel shook her head. "It's fine, Abuelo," she said. "Please sit back down."

"I need to stand," he said. "These bones need to move or they will lock up on me."

Only once she was sure her grandfather was fine did Isabel look back at the sheriff's deputy. "How does this work?" she asked. "I've never been questioned by the police before."

"Let's start at the beginning," Deputy Jackson suggested. He withdrew a small notepad and pen from the back pocket of his pants. "Walk me through your morning."

Isabel did as he requested, leaving out the fact she'd had trouble sleeping thanks to the family argument and Wyatt's return. It didn't take long to describe today's events. It helped that the deputy was such a good listener; unlike her brother, he didn't interrupt her after every other sentence.

"So it's your opinion this trap was deliberately set by someone trespassing on ranch land?"

"Yes," she replied.

"Do you think you were the target of this trap?"

It was a possibility she hadn't considered. But she quickly dismissed the suggestion. "No." She shook her head slowly. "I think I was just unlucky. Any one of the ranch workers could have found the dead cattle yesterday, or gone out to check the area today. If someone was trying to get rid of me, there are far easier ways to do it."

The deputy nodded. "I think you're right about that. So the question we need to ask is if this is an example of a prank gone wrong? Or do you think someone is trying to damage the ranch?"

Isabel glanced at her brother. Diego avoided her gaze.

The deputy caught her eye, his expression making it clear he hadn't missed a trick. "This is the time when I ask if your family has any enemies or anyone who might want to harm your business?"

"No," Diego said just as Isabel replied, "Maybe?"

Deputy Jackson smiled, though there was little humor in his expression. "Let's try that again."

Isabel ignored Diego's glare.

"You know the Praline Energy Corporation?" At the deputy's nod, she continued. "They've made an offer for our mineral rights. They want to put a fracking well on the ranch."

The lawman glanced from Diego back to her. "I take it this is a point of contention?"

Jose snorted. "Indeed."

"It would be a mistake," Diego muttered.

"It's a smart move," Isabel shot back.

The deputy lifted a hand. "I don't really need to be here for this." He faced Isabel. "Why don't you tell me why you think there's a connection between the cyanide trap and the energy company's offer?"

Isabel frowned. "I'm not positive that there is," she began. "I just have a hunch that they're behind this somehow." She looked at Diego. "We talked last night that the company was making us a good faith offer, but if we refused, they'd use other methods to try to force us to sell."

Her brother nodded. "Yeah, like eminent domain or something similar."

"Well, what if they're trying a different tack? We lost three cattle yesterday. If we start to lose more, we'll have a big problem on our hands. We'd have no choice but to sell the mineral rights."

All three men stared at her as if she'd sprouted a second head.

"That's ridiculous—" Diego began.

Deputy Jackson cut him off. "That's certainly one theory," he said smoothly. "But what you're suggesting is highly illegal and would expose the company to criminal penalties and civil lawsuits."

Isabel's heart sank as she realized none of them was taking her seriously. Even Abuelo was looking at her with pity in his eyes.

She glanced down at her lap then rubbed her forehead with her fingertips again. Maybe she was tilting at windmills. The deputy's words made a lot of sense, and he was probably right. In the grand scheme of things, their ranch was small potatoes. It was highly unlikely the energy company would engage in illegal activities for the sake of placing one fracking well.

"Right," she said softly. "I guess I'm still a little fuzzy from earlier. I must not be thinking clearly."

This time, the deputy's smile was kind. "You experienced quite an ordeal this morning. The best thing you can do is focus on your recovery. My partner and I will check things out and let you all know if we find anything." He flipped his notepad shut, a clear sign the interview was over.

Isabel didn't think his investigation would reveal much, especially since he apparently thought she was a crackpot. Nevertheless, she gave him a weak smile. "Thank you for listening to me."

"Of course, ma'am." He touched the brim of his hat. "If there's anything else you remember or think I should know, please reach out." He pulled a business card from his shirt pocket and set it on the table next to her, tapping it with his forefinger for emphasis. "That goes for any of you," he added, looking at Jose and Diego in turn. Her relatives nodded and thanked him quietly as he left the room.

Isabel felt their eyes on her once they were alone again. Their skepticism hung in the air between them, an invisible cloud she could feel but not see.

After a moment, Diego broke the silence. "I'm going to go look for Maria. Maybe she needs help finding a nurse."

When he was gone, Abuelo approached the side of her bed. He placed his hand over hers, his touch gentle.

"What is it, *mija*?"

Isabel shook her head, blinking as tears stung her eyes. "I'm not crazy," she said softly.

"Who said you were?"

"I know what you're all thinking. That I've cooked up some conspiracy theory to explain today's accident." She smeared away a tear trailing down her cheek. "But I know someone put that trap on our land deliberately. It wasn't a prank gone wrong, or a surveyor who got lost. Someone is trying to hurt us." She hadn't wanted to articulate her suspicions, but she couldn't ignore them.

Abuelo squeezed her hand. "I know."

Isabel glanced up so quickly her nasal cannula nearly fell off her face. "You do?" A flicker of hope drove back the darkness of her despair.

Her grandfather nodded. "I agree with you that this was a targeted act. But I am not so sure the energy company is behind it."

"I don't want to believe that, either. But who else could it be?"

The old man shook his head. "That, I do not know." He sighed, glancing over at the door. "Your brother can be a handful at times. He often speaks without thinking. Maybe he offended the wrong person?"

Isabel had to smile at the understatement. "That is definitely something to consider."

"But not now." Her *abuelo* used his free hand to brush a strand of hair away from her face. "Leave the worrying to me, at least for today. Take this time for yourself, to rest and recover."

"Everyone keeps telling me to rest," she muttered.

"You should listen." He smiled down at her. "Trust this old man. These troubles will still be here tomorrow. Build your strength today so you will be prepared to face them again."

It was good advice, and truth be told, Isabel was exhausted. Even though she wanted to keep going, there was a very real chance that if she tried, her body would simply revolt and force her to rest. With calving season about to start, Isabel couldn't afford to be out any longer than absolutely necessary.

"*Sí*, Abuelo," she said. If she didn't agree with him, he was liable to stick Maria on her case. That was definitely a battle she wouldn't win.

As if summoned by her thoughts, the door opened and Maria and Diego walked in together. The older woman walked to the side of the bed and placed her hand on Isabel's arm.

"I found the nurse, *mija*," she said. "She said she'll come soon with something for your head."

"Thank you."

Maria studied her face for a few seconds. "We will leave you now." She gestured to Abuelo and Diego. "She needs to sleep."

"But they are keeping her overnight," Abuelo protested. "One of us should be here."

"I can stay," Diego volunteered. "I'll take you two home and come back."

Isabel shook her head. It was kind of him to make the offer, but she didn't want her brother keeping her company in her hospital room until she was released. If they spent that much time together, they were liable to wind up in another argument, and she'd have even more headaches.

"I'll be fine," she said. "I'm going to spend most of my stay sleeping. There's no need for someone to be here watching over me."

"Are you sure?" Diego searched her features, looking for any signs of deception. Some of Isabel's annoyance faded in the face of his obvious concern. He really did love her. He just had a heavy-handed way of showing it sometimes.

"I'm positive," she assured him. "Go home. I know you all have a lot of work to do."

Diego looked down and ran a hand through his hair. "Well, yeah, that's true. My first order of business is to take care of that trap."

A stone of worry formed in her stomach. "You be careful," she ordered. "Take several men with you, and grab some of my protective gear out of the barn—gloves and face shields at the least."

"I'll be all right," he said. "Unlike *some* members of this family, I know how to handle myself around an M44." He nudged her foot with a sly grin, unable to resist teasing her. Abuelo and Maria turned in unison to glare at him. Diego's eyes went wide in an expression of mock innocence. "What?" he asked. "Too soon?"

Isabel merely shook her head, familiar with her brother's twisted sense of humor. "You might want to do a thorough search of the area. I hope that was the only trap set, but there could be more."

Diego nodded, all traces of joking gone. "That's what I'm afraid of," he said. "Why stop at one?"

The question cast a pall over the room, broken by the arrival of a nurse holding a small paper cup. "I have something for your pain," she said brightly.

She walked over to the computer system set up in the corner of the room. Abuelo leaned forward and pressed a kiss to Isabel's forehead. "Remember what we talked about," he said softly. "Rest while you can."

"Voy a dormir," she replied. *I will sleep.*

Maria squeezed her arm. "Tomorrow I will make your favorite enchiladas," she promised.

Isabel smiled. "That sounds wonderful."

Diego gave her foot an awkward pat. "Call if you need anything."

"Where is Wyatt?" Now that her family was leaving, Isabel was reminded of how she and Wyatt had arrived at the hospital. "He'll need to ride back with you."

"He was still talking to the deputies when Maria and I came back," Diego said. "I'll find out what's going on. Don't worry—we'll take care of him."

Isabel nodded. She wished she could have had more time alone with Wyatt to thank him again for saving her life. But it was probably better this way. They were never going to be more than friends who saw each other occasionally. Being around him would only cause her to become attached and make it harder for her to keep her emotions under control.

The nurse walked over as her family shuffled out. "Name and birthday, please?"

Isabel confirmed her identity and was rewarded with the small paper cup, which contained two round white pills.

"This should help with your discomfort," the nurse said, handing her the plastic cup of water Maria had recently refreshed.

"Thanks," Isabel said.

The nurse smiled. "Of course. Push the call button if you need anything else." She hurried out, leaving Isabel alone once again, with only her thoughts for company.

Two days ago, her life had seemed simple. Now it was anything but. Between the upcoming calving season, the drilling decision, the cyanide trap and, oh, yes, the reappearance of the first man she'd ever loved, things were spiraling out of control. It was enough to make her want to run away, to take an extended vacation filled with ocean waves, soft sandy beaches and colorful drinks sporting tiny paper umbrellas. Just thinking about it made her head spin pleasantly.

No, wait. Her clinical training kicked in. *Those are the drugs.* Whatever the nurse had given her was working. Her headache was receding as a warm, fuzzy sensation stole over her. She felt curiously lightweight, as though she might float off the bed at any moment.

For a few seconds, her mind struggled to hold on to her worries and concerns. But it was no use—one by one, her thoughts slipped out of her grasp, her consciousness a boat shrugging off the moorings of logic. With a sigh, Isabel closed her eyes and surrendered to the inevitable.

She's so beautiful.

Wyatt sat in the chair next to Isabel's bed, watching her sleep. There was nothing especially entertaining about the sight, but for some reason he couldn't tear his eyes away from her.

The deputies had finished questioning him a couple of hours ago. He'd turned down Diego's offer of a ride back to the ranch—at the time, he was still talking to the lawmen.

"I know a few park rangers who live in Alpine," he'd told Diego. "I'll call one of them and catch a ride back to the park tomorrow morning." He'd already called in and asked for time off to deal with a family emergency, so there was no rush for him to return to the park.

It was the truth, and at the time, Wyatt had intended to duck into Isabel's room, say goodbye and then connect with one of his fellow rangers. But she'd looked so peaceful he'd found himself sinking into the chair, wanting to be near her. The sounds of her steady breathing soaked into his chest and calmed his still frayed nerves.

As a park ranger, he'd elected to pursue additional training in medical emergencies and basic rescues. A lot of Big Bend was remote wilderness, making it hard to get help to the visitors who might need it. He'd encountered hikers and campers with problems ranging in severity from sprained ankles to heart attacks and heat stroke. He'd handled them all without missing a beat, never letting his emotions get involved. But this morning's accident had been different.

And he wasn't going to try to pretend that he didn't know the reason why.

His heart had skipped a beat when he'd clapped eyes on the cyanide trap and recognized it for what it was. Fortunately, his training had kicked in a moment later, the autopilot taking over and allowing him to function. It was the only reason he'd been able to help Isabel. If he'd actually stopped to think about what was happening, he would have been too upset to be effective. His only regret was that he'd not pulled her back from the peril more quickly.

Even now, hours after the fact, it rattled him to think about how things could have turned out. If he had gotten to her a few minutes later, if Ajax hadn't made it back to the house so fast, if the medevac hadn't arrived when it did—any number of seemingly small factors could have changed the outcome, leaving her dead and him heartbroken.

And he would have been heartbroken, no doubt about it. Regardless of how their romantic interlude had ended a decade ago, he still cared about her. They'd spent too much time together while growing up to simply dismiss her from his life.

But now that she was back, his general affection was in danger of sliding into something decidedly less platonic. It was a pitfall he would do well to avoid, since they would probably see each other on a regular basis.

One thing he did know: sitting here in the fading light of the afternoon watching Isabel sleep was no way to keep his emotions in check.

With that in mind, Wyatt placed his hands on the armrests of the chair and began to push himself up. The Naugahyde cushions squeaked in protest at the movement and, to his horror, Isabel stirred.

He froze, half in and half out of the chair, and cursed silently. The last thing he'd wanted to do was to wake her. She might not appreciate finding him in her hospital room, especially since he knew his opposition to the drilling proposal had hurt her feelings.

Moving carefully, Wyatt unfolded to his full height, wincing as the chair provided an unwelcome soundtrack for his every movement. He eyed the expanse of linoleum stretching out before him, knowing the heels of his boots would clop as he walked. Why was the damn door so far away?

He made it a few steps before Isabel's voice stopped him in his tracks.

"Wyatt?"

She sounded fuzzy, likely a combination of the aftereffects of the cyanide and her nap. He turned around with an apologetic half smile.

"I'm sorry. I didn't mean to wake you."

Isabel rubbed her eyes with one hand and used the other to fish for the bed controls amid the thin sheet and blankets. The metal frame made a soft whirring sound as she raised the head of the mattress, allowing her to sit up with relative comfort.

"It's no problem. You didn't, really. At least, I don't think you did." He could see the mental fog clear as she looked at him. "Why did you come back?"

"I never actually left," he confessed.

"You didn't?" She frowned. "But I asked Diego to give you a ride back to the ranch. He told me he'd take care of you." Her tone changed, making it clear she wasn't happy with her brother.

Uh-oh, Wyatt thought. He didn't want to contribute to any misunderstandings between Isabel and Diego. If last night's conversation in Jose's study was any indication, the siblings already had enough to argue about.

"He did offer, but I turned him down," he said. "I was still being questioned by the deputies, and I wasn't sure how much longer that was going to take. I didn't want to ask them to wait for me, especially with so much work to be done at the ranch."

"Oh." She frowned. "Deputy Jackson was only

here for a few minutes. I wonder why they were so interested in talking to you?"

Wyatt shrugged. "I think they wanted to make sure my recounting of the events matched up with yours." They had also spent a fair bit of time asking Wyatt how he'd known what the trap was after catching only a glimpse of it in the dirt, and if he could account for his whereabouts over the past few days. The deputies hadn't accused him of anything outright, but it was clear they were questioning if his presence at the ranch was a mere coincidence or something more sinister.

Wyatt wasn't worried for himself—it would take a matter of minutes to prove he had nothing to do with this. He just hoped the deputies would apply the same level of skepticism to the rest of the investigation and actually attempt to find out who was responsible for setting the trap, rather than writing it off as a wild-goose chase.

"I guess that makes sense." She didn't look satisfied, though. He could tell from her expression she was working something out in her head, so he didn't respond.

After a few seconds, she sighed quietly. "Do you think they're taking this seriously?"

"Hard to say." Wyatt returned to the chair and sat. "The fact that you were hurt this morning makes this more than just a routine case of trespassing. But they definitely have their work cut out for them. There are no witnesses, and I doubt they're going to try to get fingerprints off the trap."

"I told them I thought the energy company might have something to do with it. The deputy, Diego and Abuelo all looked at me like I was crazy." She shook her head. "But I know there's something going on here. I just can't put my finger on what it is."

Her suggestion gave him pause. Wyatt had already concluded the trap had been deliberately set and baited. Someone had walked onto ranch land with the intention of killing Cruz cattle. But he hadn't thought the energy company was behind this. For Isabel to wonder about that, when she'd previously been interested in talking to the company about selling mineral rights, gave the idea more weight. "What makes you think the company is involved?"

"The timing of it is awfully strange, don't you think?"

"How so?"

"They made the initial offer almost two weeks ago. They came out to pester Abuelo again yesterday afternoon, offering an extension for more time to consider it. Maybe they're trying to nudge us into saying yes by targeting our cattle. If we lose our animals, we lose our livelihood. We'd need a new source of income, and here they are, ready to give us a wad of cash in exchange for a few signatures."

Wyatt's first instinct was to dismiss the possibility. What Isabel was suggesting was illegal. Surely a company wouldn't take that kind of risk?

But one look at her face made him bite his tongue. He could tell she was frustrated, but there was a hint of vulnerability in her eyes that touched his heart. Her brother, grandfather and the deputy sheriff had all dismissed her suggestion—even despite Diego's antipathy toward the company—which had likely left her feeling even more alone. Wyatt wasn't sure if he agreed with her suspicions, but he didn't want her to feel unheard.

"It's possible," he said slowly.

"But you don't think it's true." Isabel nodded, as if she'd expected his reaction.

He leaned forward, wanting to be closer to her. "I'm not sure. It's a good theory, but it'll be incredibly difficult to prove."

"Yeah." It was hard to miss the note of discouragement in her voice. Wyatt reached out and covered her hand with his own. When she looked at him, he offered her a smile. "I know I supported the idea of selling mineral rights, but that doesn't mean I'm blind to how these companies work," she said.

"I know. I said it would be difficult to prove. Not impossible."

A ghost of a smile flickered across her face. "Does that mean you'll help me?"

Wyatt nodded without a second thought. "As best I can."

Isabel flipped her hand under his so they were palm to palm. She threaded her fingers through his and squeezed.

The gesture was surprisingly intimate. Electric tingles shot up Wyatt's arm as latent nerve endings sparked to life. He stared at their linked hands, wondering if Isabel was trying to tell him something, or if he was merely projecting his own hopes on to a simple gesture.

There was only one way to find out.

He took a deep breath and spoke before he lost his nerve. "Can I ask you a question?"

"Sure."

"Why did you leave without saying goodbye?"

He didn't have to clarify anything. As soon as he'd said the words, Isabel's face went carefully blank. She didn't respond right away and the silence stretched between them, growing heavier with each passing second.

"I suppose we do need to talk about that," she said finally.

Tension coiled within his chest. Wyatt felt like he was standing on a precipice, his toes hanging over the edge. This conversation was ten years in the making. And while he'd imagined it many times in his mind, now that the actual moment had arrived, he wasn't sure he was ready.

"Look, if you regret what we did that night, or if you feel like I pressured you…" Wyatt had been careful to ask Isabel if she was okay several times during their encounter, and she'd said yes. But perhaps she'd only been telling him what he had wanted to hear?

Isabel held up her hand. "I don't think that now,

and I didn't at the time, either. I knew what I was doing, and you didn't take advantage of me."

Wyatt exhaled, relief stealing over him. The thought that Isabel had felt forced or otherwise been uncomfortable had haunted him for some time, gnawing away at his soul and causing him to question his memories of that night. Her reassurances alleviated his worries and gave him permission to look back on that night with pleasure instead of a vague sense of guilt.

But if she hadn't been upset about sleeping with him, then what had caused her abrupt change in attitude?

"I don't understand," he began. "Why did you—"

"Because I saw you the next day," Isabel said, interrupting him. There was an edge to her voice now that told him they were getting to the heart of the matter. She leveled an accusatory stare at him, practically daring him to say something.

Wyatt racked his brain, trying to figure out what he'd done the next day that she'd found so offensive. Hell, he hadn't even *seen* Isabel then. He'd spent the morning at home, then gone into town in search of a new pair of jeans to take back to school. He'd hoped to take Isabel to dinner that night, but she hadn't answered his calls.

Isabel rolled her eyes, apparently frustrated by his lack of response. "I saw you," she repeated again, speaking slowly. "With Nikki."

All at once, the pieces tumbled into place. "Oh," he said dumbly.

He'd run into Nikki while in town. She'd asked about his plans for the night and he'd explained he was busy. Sensing something was going on, she'd pressed him for information. Wyatt had confessed he had feelings for someone else and that he didn't want to see her romantically again. Nikki hadn't wanted to give up so easily, though. Before he'd known what was happening, Nikki had grabbed him and pressed her body against his, kissing him hard as she'd tried to convince him to change his mind.

Wyatt didn't know what they'd looked like to passersby, but if Isabel's reaction was any indication, his discomfort with Nikki's actions must not have been obvious.

"You remember now, don't you?" Isabel asked softly.

"Yeah," he replied. He withdrew his hand, moved it down his face. What he wouldn't give to go back in time and change things! Instead of talking to Nikki, he'd turn around and walk away. It was mind-boggling that one simple choice had made such a drastic impact on his life.

He met Isabel's stare, expecting to find anger or disappointment there. Instead he saw a faint sadness in her brown gaze.

"It's okay," she said simply. "It was silly of me to assume you had feelings for me after one night together."

"No, it wasn't," he said quietly. Her eyes widened slightly, a question forming on her lips. "I care about you," he said, deciding to take the plunge and dive in. "I always have. That night meant a lot to me. I had hoped it was the start of something between us." He leaned back in the chair, tilted his head to the side. "I didn't run off to Nikki the next day. I bumped into her while I was shopping for clothes to take back to college. I told her I didn't want to date her any more. What you saw was her attempt at changing my mind."

Isabel's lips parted but no sound came out. A parade of emotions marched across her face: doubt, uncertainty, acceptance, frustration and regret. "My God," she finally whispered. "I was so wrapped up in my own hurt that I never thought there might be another explanation for what I'd seen."

He gave her a lopsided smile. "Can't say I blame you. If our roles had been reversed, I would have been angry, too."

She blinked, her eyes shiny as she looked at him. "You tried to contact me…"

Wyatt nodded. "Now I know why you never answered."

They stared at each other, both trying to process these revelations and decide what they meant for themselves. For his part, Wyatt was relieved to find Isabel didn't hate him or feel like he'd used her. But he was heartsick over the misunderstanding that had changed the course of their relationship.

How different would things be between them now if Isabel had seen him a few minutes before he'd encountered Nikki, or a few minutes after he'd extricated himself from her embrace? Would they still be together, perhaps even married with children and a dog? Or would they have eventually parted ways, heading in separate directions to chase their dreams? Either way, he felt certain they would have at least taken a chance on each other.

Wyatt glanced out the window, so occupied with his thoughts he didn't really see anything outside. He was glad to finally know why Isabel had suddenly pulled away from him, but now he felt cheated out of the past ten years of his life.

"I don't know what to think," she said. He turned back to find Isabel shaking her head. "I was angry with you for a long time. But I couldn't stay mad at you forever—there were too many good memories of the three of us growing up together, you know?"

Wyatt nodded. "I do, yes." It was the same reason he'd let go of his own hurt after she'd cut him off with no explanation.

"I made my peace with it," she continued. "That's why I was able to move back here, knowing I would see you again. But now I feel like I'm in a bad reality TV show." She let out a sound that might have been a laugh. "If this is the universe's idea of a joke, it's not very funny."

"I wish…" Wyatt began. He let the thought trail off. "Well, there's a lot of things I wish were different. Doesn't matter, though. It won't change anything."

"Where do we go from here?" she asked softly.

It was the only question, wasn't it? They couldn't go back in time, couldn't relive those years. The only thing they could do was choose how to move forward.

"I'm not sure," he confessed. He was definitely still attracted to Isabel—that hadn't changed in the time they'd been apart. But while in some ways he felt like he still knew her, in other ways she was a stranger. A decade was a long time to go without talking to one another. They certainly weren't the same kids they'd once been. Would it be a mistake to assume they could simply pick up where they'd left off?

But…given the time they'd already lost, would it be a bigger mistake to pass up this opportunity to reconnect?

"Where do you want to go?" he asked. Hope tingled in his chest. The more he thought about it, the more he wanted to find out if they were compatible. He refused to think the encounter in the bed of his pickup truck was the high point of their relationship.

Isabel didn't answer right away. She ran her hands over the thin hospital blanket, smoothing out invisible wrinkles. Finally she looked up at him, her eyes twinkling.

"Why don't we just drive around for a bit?" she said, echoing what she'd suggested to him ten years ago.

Chapter 7

Isabel blinked at the morning sun as the orderly wheeled her out of the hospital. She'd wanted to walk, but the orderly had insisted she ride.

"It's hospital policy," the woman had said with a smile, locking the wheelchair into position so Isabel could sit.

They came to a stop at the edge of the paved entrance, next to the patient drop-off and pick-up lane. The woman locked the wheels again, apparently prepared to wait with her until Diego arrived.

"Can I stand up now?" Isabel asked.

"Yes, of course."

She pushed herself out of the chair, happy to be on her feet after spending the day in bed yesterday.

"Do you need me to wait with you?" the orderly asked.

Isabel shook her head. "No, thank you. I'll be all right. I have company." She slid a glance over to Wyatt, who smiled.

The woman looked from her to Wyatt and back again. "Very good. You take care."

"Thank you."

The orderly unlocked the wheelchair and pushed it back into the hospital, leaving the two of them alone. Wyatt inclined his head at a bench a few feet from the entrance. "Shall we?"

Isabel nodded, following him over to sit on the pebbled stone surface. The bench was long, but by mutual unspoken agreement, they sat so close to each other their bodies touched, creating an unbroken line of warmth that ran from her shoulder to her knee. She reached for his hand, linking their fingers in a gesture that felt as natural as breathing.

Wyatt had stayed with her last night. It wasn't anything they had planned, but once they'd started talking, they hadn't wanted to stop. They'd spent the night catching up on each other's lives. Isabel had told him stories from college and vet school, and described some of her more outrageous cases. He'd told her about becoming a park ranger, and the special medical and rescue training he'd completed. She'd held her breath as he'd told her about some of the rescues he'd been involved with, and her heart had pounded as he'd described encounters with the wildlife in the park.

She hadn't ever thought about the details of a park ranger's job before—part of her had assumed it was like a daily nature walk, a fun way to spend time outside. But Wyatt's stories made her realize the job was far more interesting—and dangerous—than that.

The conversation had flowed easily, a connection she didn't take for granted. Learning the truth about what she'd seen ten years ago had been a shock and part of her still felt guilty for allowing her anger to rule her response. If she'd picked up the phone just once, listened to him explain everything, they might not have lost all that time. But her logical mind knew there was no sense dwelling in the past and torturing herself with the might-have-beens. Better to focus on the here and now. They'd been given a second chance. Now that she knew how he really felt about her, she intended to take it.

"Are you sure you're feeling up to going home?"

Isabel smiled and rested her head on Wyatt's shoulder. "Yeah. There's a lot of work to be done. I can't leave it all for Diego."

"Fair enough," Wyatt said ruefully. "But you can't blame me for worrying."

She gave his hand a squeeze. "At the risk of sounding crazy, I did kind of enjoy my time here."

"I did, too," he said quietly.

Isabel pulled away slightly and looked up at him, staring into those bright blue eyes that never failed to make her breath catch. Being confined to a hospital bed wasn't her idea of fun, but the time she and Wyatt had spent together had been wonderful. For a few hours, they had blocked out the world and focused only on each other. The emotional distance between them had melted away, bringing them closer than ever before. There were still a lot of things they had to figure out, but Isabel was confident they were heading in the right direction.

Together.

His gaze was warm, making her skin tingle as anticipation and desire thrummed through her. They'd only talked last night. Perhaps it was time to do something more?

Wyatt leaned forward, closing the distance between them. Isabel's stomach fluttered as his scent filled her nose—soap, coffee and the faint twinge of horses left over from yesterday's events. Her tongue darted out to moisten her lips and her eyes drifted shut as he moved closer.

But a few seconds later she opened them again to find Wyatt staring down at her.

"Are you teasing me?" she accused.

"I didn't mean to," he said. "But it's been so long since we were this close. I guess I was waiting for you to change your mind."

"You'll be waiting awhile," she murmured. She lifted her hand to his cheek, pulling him closer.

The kiss was hesitant at first, a brush of lips and a whisper of breath. His whiskers scraped across her chin in a soft tickle that set off sparks low in her belly. Wyatt's arms circled around her, pulling her body against him. Her breasts flattened against the hard planes of his chest, creating a delicious pressure that sent a wave of heat though her.

All at once, she was back in the bed of his pickup, her body begging for more of his touch. How was it that one kiss from this man set her self-control on fire and made her desperate for more? She'd long ago attributed their physical chemistry to the effects of teenage hormones. But as he deepened the kiss, making her head spin, she realized just how wrong she'd been.

Wyatt was intoxicating, like her own personal drug. Would she ever get enough?

Let's find out, her hormones suggested, happy to throw propriety to the wind. Fortunately, Isabel retained enough awareness to remember they were in public and after a brief internal struggle, she pulled back, breaking the contact between them.

Wyatt's eyes were wide with a wild gleam that she was certain mirrored her own gaze. He dropped his forehead to hers, their breaths mingling as the intensity of the moment faded.

"That was…" he began, his voice rough. "Wow."

Isabel laughed softly. "Took the words out of my mouth."

He grinned suggestively. "I'm happy to carry on that kind of conversation with you any time."

Her fingers itched to pull him close again, but she

fought the urge. Diego would be here soon and she didn't want her brother to find them making out like horny teenagers.

"Maybe later," she said. "We'll need some privacy before we talk again."

His answering smile was full of promise, lighting a flame of anticipation in her chest. Isabel was tempted to drag Wyatt back into the hospital and find an empty room so they could pick up where they'd left off. But the familiar rumble of a truck engine put a damper on her arousal.

Diego pulled to a stop and rolled down the passenger-side window. "Hey, man," he called. "Thought your friend was gonna give you a ride?"

Isabel and Wyatt headed for the truck. He opened the back door and she slid inside, scooting behind Diego so Wyatt had room next to her.

"He was busy," Wyatt said. "I kept your sister company instead."

Diego made a low sound of dissatisfaction. "And now you guys are riding in the back like I'm your damn chauffeur?"

Isabel grinned. "Home, Jeeves," she commanded.

"Whatever," he grumbled. The truck shot forward, pushing Isabel back into the seat as she buckled her seat belt.

"Did you have any trouble disposing of the trap yesterday?" she asked.

"No," Diego responded. He lifted his eyes to the

rearview mirror then returned his gaze to the road. "But it wasn't a normal trap."

"What do you mean?" Wyatt leaned forward, the seat belt tightening across his chest as he moved.

"It's hard to describe," Diego said. "You know how a normal M44 works?"

Wyatt nodded, but Isabel frowned. "I don't," she said, not wanting to be left out of the conversation.

"It targets coyotes and wild dogs," Wyatt said, turning to face her. "The trap is baited with meat tied to the tube. When the coyote bites and pulls, the pressure of it triggers a spray of cyanide into the animal's mouth."

"Oh." She wrinkled her nose. "That sounds terrible."

"It is," Wyatt said shortly. "But very effective."

"The thing is," Diego interjected, "these traps usually require a pretty forceful tug to fire. It's kind of a safety mechanism—you wouldn't want a stiff breeze or a sniff by a curious animal to set it off. But the one we pulled out of the ground yesterday was missing some parts. I think it was modified so that it would release the cyanide when a cow nibbled at it."

A chill skittered down Isabel's spine. "So not only did someone deliberately put this on our land, they made sure it would target our cows."

"Yeah," Diego confirmed.

"Did you tell the deputies?" Wyatt asked.

"We did," Diego said. "They came out to the ranch

and collected it, said they would send it to El Paso for testing."

"Like for fingerprints?" Isabel asked.

"I guess. And to figure out how it had been altered. Maybe someone's done this before and is in their system?"

It was a long shot, but possible. "Let's hope so," she murmured.

"Did you find any other traps?" Wyatt asked.

"No," Diego said.

"That doesn't mean they're not there," Isabel pointed out. She glanced out the window at the landscape as it raced by. In the distance, she could see the tall, white-metal towers of the fracking wells that dotted the area. Was there a connection between the energy company and the cyanide trap? Or were her brother and the detective right, and she was letting her imagination get the better of her? Her brother, after all, had more motivation to think the worst of the company. He didn't want to sell to them.

She was quiet for the rest of the trip, happy to listen to Wyatt and Diego talk. Their easy banter hadn't changed and she enjoyed hearing them tease each other even as they discussed serious topics.

When they turned onto the private road that connected the ranch to the rest of the world, Isabel leaned forward. It looked like the main herd was grazing on the west pasture today. The animals were too far away for her to make out any individuals.

"Any calving last night?" she asked.

"No," Diego said. "But we kept a few heifers close to the barn today, just in case."

"Good call," she said. Most cows gave birth to their first calf without incident. But sometimes a mama needed help getting her baby out. There was no way to know ahead of time which animals would require assistance, so it was common practice to keep the inexperienced cows close to the barn as their pregnancy wound down.

She saw the animals as they drove past the barn, a small group of brown cows with rounded sides and swollen udders. Diego slowed to give her a better look as they drove past. Most of the animals looked good, but there was one standing by herself in the far end of the small pasture.

"She's gonna go soon," Isabel said, pointing to the loner.

Diego glanced out his window, nodded. "You're probably right," he replied.

"How do you know?" Wyatt asked. He'd unbuckled his seat belt and was now behind her, leaning forward for a better look. Isabel relaxed against him, enjoying the feel of him at her back.

"She's off by herself," Isabel said. "And I bet when I get a closer look at her, she'll be dilating."

"Are you going to let things happen naturally or will you help her?"

"I'm not going to interfere unless she needs assistance. I prefer to stay out of the way if possible."

"How do you even help deliver a calf?" Wyatt mused.

Diego laughed. "It's a lot of pulling."

"Definitely a workout," Isabel confirmed.

"Don't you remember watching a calving when we were in high school?" Diego asked. "You were here when one of the cows delivered. It was twins."

"Yeah, I know," Wyatt answered, sounding a little defensive. "But if I recall correctly, I stood at the edge of the fence and watched. We didn't have to do anything."

"*You* didn't," Diego shot back. "But Abuelo made sure I stayed busy. As usual."

"Kept you out of trouble, didn't it?"

Isabel smiled to herself, knowing Wyatt was right. Abuelo was no fool—he'd always been a few steps ahead of Diego. Keeping her brother busy was the key to managing him.

Diego made a dismissive sound. "Whatever." He parked next to the house and cut the engine.

Isabel opened the door and slid to the ground, the gravel crunching under her boots. She walked around the bed of the truck to where Wyatt was standing. Together, they moved toward the porch steps.

Just as Isabel put her foot on the first step, the front door swung open and Maria flew out. "*¡Mija!*" She hurried over and wrapped her arms around Isabel, squeezing so tightly Isabel couldn't breathe. "How are you feeling? You still look pale. Should you still be in the hospital?"

Isabel smiled at the onslaught of questions. "I feel fine. I don't need to be in the hospital any longer—there's nothing more the doctors need to do for me."

Maria arched one eyebrow, clearly skeptical. "Did they feed you there?"

Isabel knew the correct answer for this one. "Yes. But it wasn't nearly as good as your cooking."

"Of course not." Maria sniffed, her chin lifting in pride. "Homemade food is always better. Come inside now, I have lunch ready for you." She took Isabel's arm and began to lead her toward the door. "You, too, Wyatt," Maria called over her shoulder.

"*Gracias,* Tía," he said.

"What about me?" Diego asked.

"Since when do you need an invitation?"

Her brother grinned and started to follow. Just as they all reached the door, a low rumble sounded from the direction of the main road, growing steadily louder. Someone was on the way to the ranch house and getting closer.

Isabel paused on the threshold. "Are we expecting anyone?"

Diego shook his head. "Not that I know of."

The four of them watched an older model truck bounce down the road, past the barn and alongside the calving pasture. The driver pulled up next to Diego's truck and cut the engine.

Isabel frowned. She didn't recognize the vehicle or the man driving it. She glanced at Diego and gathered from his puzzled expression that he didn't know him, either.

"Who is that?" Maria asked softly.

The man climbed out of his truck and shut the door. He stood there for a second, surveying the land with a proprietary air before turning his gaze to the house.

There was something about his manner that rubbed Isabel the wrong way. He sauntered over to the porch, planted one foot on the second step and leaned forward as though he owned the place.

"Can I help you?" Diego's words were friendly but his tone was guarded.

Isabel felt a brush against her arm as Wyatt positioned himself slightly in front of her, with Maria behind both of them.

The man took off his sunglasses, revealing deep-set dark brown eyes. He looked to be about thirty and his brown hair was a bit on the longish side. His khaki pants were pressed, his polo shirt tucked in under a brown leather belt. His dun-colored hat was spotless, the absence of sweat stains indicating it was worn for fashion and not practicality. He looked like a stereotypical office worker, but there was something about his eyes that gave Isabel pause...

The man glanced around, clearly in no hurry to answer Diego's question. He looked from Isabel to Wyatt and craned his neck to get a better glance at Maria. Then he returned his attention to her brother.

"You're Diego Cruz?"

"That depends on who's asking."

"My name is Gabriel Richardson." He stared hard at Diego, searching for a reaction. When none came, he nodded to himself as if he'd just received confirmation of a long-held suspicion.

"What's your business here, Gabriel?" Isabel said. He wasn't from one of their suppliers—he would have identified himself as such. He wasn't from the bank, either. Was he bringing them a message from Praline Energy? He didn't fit the slick-suited image of the other men from the company, but that didn't mean much.

The stranger looked her over, eyeing her up and down in a blatant assessment that made her blood boil. She stepped forward. Wyatt placed his hand on her shoulder and squeezed, though whether in reassurance or warning, she wasn't sure.

"I'm here to meet the family," he drawled.

"Isabel? I thought that was you." Abuelo's voice drifted out of the house. She sensed his presence behind her but didn't turn around. "What are you all doing standing on the porch?"

Gabriel craned his head, searching past the scrum for Abuelo's face. When he saw the older man, he broke into a wide grin that sent a chill down Isabel's spine.

"Hello, Grandpa."

Everything happened fast.

Gabriel's words hit like a bomb. Wyatt heard Jose

suck in a breath. He reflexively turned, reaching out to put a steadying hand on the older man's shoulder.

Maria whispered a curse, her brows drawn together and her expression fierce.

But it was Diego's reaction that worried him the most.

"The hell you say!" His friend took a step forward, the movement menacing. "I don't know what kind of game you're playing, but you're not welcome here. Leave, now."

Seemingly unaware of the danger he was in, Gabriel smirked. "I have every right to be here."

"Get off of our property," Diego seethed. "Before I make you."

"No."

Isabel darted forward, grabbing her brother's arm before he could take a swing. Wyatt hastily entrusted Jose to Maria's care. "Take him inside," he instructed. Then he moved to stand at Diego's other side. In their long friendship, he'd only seen Diego punch someone once before. But unless he missed his guess, Wyatt figured he was about to witness a second incident.

"It's fine," Isabel said forcefully. "Everybody, go inside."

Gabriel lifted himself onto the second step of the porch.

"Not you." The look Isabel gave the man was capable of stripping paint. "You can stay here and wait for the police."

Gabriel shrugged, clearly unfazed by the threat. "That'll take hours."

"I have a better solution." Diego no longer looked like he was going to hit the man, but Wyatt could feel the leashed tension in his friend's body and knew that if he loosened his grip, Diego might go on the attack. "You're trespassing on private property. I'd be well within my rights to shoot you."

Isabel looked shocked at her brother's suggestion.

Wyatt clenched his jaw. *Way to escalate things, buddy.* Diego could always be counted on to act rashly.

"Well, see, that's the thing," Gabriel replied. "I'm not trespassing. This is Cruz land." He paused, stared hard at Diego in a clear challenge. "And I'm a Cruz."

Wyatt threw his arm across Diego's shoulders, hauling him back as his friend lunged. His boot heels began to slide on the boards of the porch, which were worn smooth from years of traffic. Wyatt had a few inches on his friend, but Diego was two hundred and thirty pounds of pure, pissed-off muscle. Unless someone or something broke through the red haze of Diego's anger, Wyatt wasn't going to be able to hold him back much longer.

He glanced at Isabel. She nodded, correctly interpreting his expression. She moved out of his sight for a second and returned with Maria's dish towel in her hands. Wyatt didn't like her being so close to her brother when he was in a rage like this, but right now he needed all the help he could get. From the corner of his vision, he saw her wrap the towel around her hands, stretching the fabric taut between them. Worst case scenario, she could throw it around her brother's head and pull back. Some mild choking should recalibrate Diego's priorities…

In the end, salvation came from an unlikely source.

"He's right." Jose's voice cut through the noise and the drama. The patriarch stepped forward, placed his hand on Diego's arm. His grandson stilled at the touch and turned to look at him, eyes wide with disbelief.

"Come inside," Jose said. He turned and started walking toward the door. "All of you," he threw over his shoulder.

Maria immediately followed.

Isabel gave Wyatt a questioning look. At his nod, she trailed after her grandfather.

Wyatt kept a restraining hand on Diego's chest. "Come on, man," he said, his voice low. "Let's go."

"I don't want him in my house."

"You would ignore grandfather's request?" Gabriel climbed the porch steps, pausing at the top.

"He is not your grandfather." Diego's face was a mottled red and his muscles trembled with barely leashed violence.

Gabriel lifted one eyebrow and a shock of recognition traveled through Wyatt. He'd seen that expression before on Isabel's face. Diego wasn't going to like it, but whoever this man was, he had some kind of connection to the Cruz family.

Gabriel opened his mouth to respond.

"Don't be stupid," Wyatt advised. "Just get in the damn house."

To his surprise, the other man did just that. He breezed past Diego without a second glance, leaving Wyatt and his friend alone on the porch.

"What are you doing?" Diego shrugged off Wyatt's grip. "Where do you get off telling him to go inside?"

"I didn't," Wyatt replied evenly. "Jose did."

"He doesn't have the right—"

"Maybe not," Wyatt interrupted. "But standing out here arguing was getting nowhere. Abuelo seems to recognize him. Why don't you go inside and find out how that's possible?"

Diego's eyes held a mutinous gleam, his temper still in control of his brain.

"Fine," Wyatt said, realizing his friend wasn't going to respond to reason. "Stay out here and be mad. I'm not going to leave Isabel and Maria alone in there with him." At that, he turned on his heel and stalked into the house.

Diego muttered a few choice words and stomped in after him.

Wyatt slowed his pace, giving his friend a chance to catch up. Together, they headed for the study.

"Are you going to be cool about this?" Wyatt kept his voice low as they approached the room. If

Diego lost his temper again, Wyatt wasn't sure he could hold him back. People would get hurt, and if Isabel was one of them, he knew he'd turn on his best friend. It was a possibility he didn't want to consider.

"Yeah." The wild look was fading from Diego's eyes, replaced by a cold calculation. "Let's go find out what this bastard wants."

Chapter 8

Abuelo sank into his desk chair, his face ashen. His hand trembled slightly as he gestured for Gabriel to take a seat.

Gabriel gave a polite nod and settled into the old recliner. Now that he was inside, away from Diego, he seemed calmer, less volatile.

Isabel lowered herself onto the ancient love seat, balancing on the edge of the cushion. She wanted to be able to move, if the occasion called for it. Wyatt had done an admirable job restraining Diego on the porch, but the study was a much smaller space. A tussle in here would be disastrous.

She heard the clomp of approaching boots and tensed. Diego appeared in the doorway, glowering at them all. She looked past her brother, relieved to see Wyatt's tall form appear. He caught her eye and nodded, offering her a tight smile.

"Don't stand there all day," Jose said, his voice tired. "Join us so we can talk."

Diego stepped into the room but made no move to come any closer. He leaned against the wall next to the door, arms crossed over his chest and his expression forbidding.

Wyatt entered next. After an assessing glance at her brother, he moved to the love seat and took the empty spot at her side. Isabel relaxed slightly. She drew comfort from Wyatt's presence, but having him here also meant reinforcements in case Diego lost his head.

Maria slipped out of the room, quietly closing the door behind her. Isabel felt a pang of jealousy and wished she could escape, as well, leaving the men alone to their testosterone together.

Jose let out a deep breath. "Gabriel," he said quietly. "What brings you here today?"

"You."

Isabel glanced at Abuelo's face, but he showed no response to Gabriel's declaration.

After a few seconds, Gabriel continued. "You're my grandfather."

"He's not your family," Diego practically growled.

Gabriel turned to look at Diego for the first time since they'd all settled in the study. "You're wrong," he said calmly. "And I can prove it." He cocked his hip off the chair cushion, pulled something from his back pocket that turned out to be a small square of paper. He unfolded it carefully, stood and walked over to place it on Abuelo's desk. Then he returned to the recliner.

As Abuelo examined the paper, his face lost what little color it had. He jerked his head up to look at Gabriel, who nodded once.

"What?" Diego demanded. "What is that?"

When Abuelo didn't immediately reply, Gabriel spoke up. "Do you want to tell him or should I?"

Jose leaned back in his chair and ran a hand down his face. "Go ahead," he said, his voice barely more than a whisper. "It's your story."

Gabriel nodded again and took a deep breath. "My mother was Christine Richardson. Ricardo Cruz was my father."

Diego made a dismissive sound in his throat, but Isabel wasn't so quick to respond. She studied Gabriel's face, the faint tingle of recognition she'd felt on the porch growing stronger as she mentally compared him with her memories of her father.

"It's true," Gabriel said, glancing at Diego. "My mother and Ricardo were together in the summer of 1982. When she realized she was pregnant, she came here to talk to him. He wasn't home. But you were." His head swiveled back to Jose.

Abuelo swallowed. "Yes, I was."

"You told her Ricardo was married, that he'd never leave his wife. You gave her that check—" he nodded at the paper on the table "—and sent her on her way."

Isabel stared at her grandfather, trying to imagine the scene. Diego's birthday was August fourteenth. If Gabriel's story was true—and the more she stared at him, the more she was certain it was—his mother would have discovered her pregnancy right around the time of Diego's birth.

"Yes," Jose repeated. "I did."

"Are you kidding me?" Diego exclaimed. He stalked over to Abuelo's desk and grabbed the check. After inspecting it for a moment, he threw it down and turned to their grandfather. "Some woman shows up pregnant and claiming Dad's the father and you believed her?" He shook his head. "Way to stand by your own son."

Anger flashed in Jose's eyes as he stared up at Diego. "I'm not a fool, young man. I'm not now and I wasn't then, either. She was telling the truth."

A flicker of doubt danced across Diego's face. "But that would mean…"

Abuelo nodded. "Your father was a complicated man. He loved you and your sister. I think he loved your mother, as best as he could. But fidelity proved too much of a challenge for him."

Her grandfather's words landed like small stones against Isabel's heart. She'd been a young girl when her parents had died in a car accident. She had many happy memories of them as individuals, but she remembered the times they'd been together as being strained, with a current of tension arcing between her mother and father. A few times they'd argued in front of her, voices loud and passions high.

Isabel had never asked Abuelo or Maria about her parents' marriage, preferring instead to focus on the good times they'd shared. But with his simple statement, Abuelo had confirmed one of her longest-held suspicions as fact.

Wyatt's arm wrapped around her, a silent gesture of support that reminded her she wasn't alone. She leaned against his side, grateful for his strength.

No one said anything for a moment. Then Diego nodded at the check. "So you gave her the money for an abortion?"

Jose nodded. "That's what she asked me to do." He turned to Gabriel. "Your mother was hurt and angry when I told her Ricardo had a wife and a newborn. She said she couldn't take care of a baby on her own, and that her family would disown her if they knew she was pregnant. She asked me to help her pay for a termination."

"So you did." Isabel couldn't keep the note of judgment from her tone. This was a side of Abuelo she'd never seen before, never even thought existed. How was it possible that the man who had rocked her back to sleep after a nightmare, gently tended to her skinned knees and sipped imaginary tea with her from tiny china cups had written a check to pay for a young woman's abortion?

Abuelo met her eyes. She saw sadness and regret

in his gaze. "Yes," he replied. "To my shame, I did what she asked."

"She changed her mind." They all turned to look at Gabriel. He lifted one shoulder in a shrug. "Obviously," he said with a lopsided grin.

At his lighter tone, the tension in the room broke. Wyatt laughed softly, Isabel did the same. Even Diego cracked a smile.

"So why are you here?" The bluster had left Diego's voice, replaced with a note of curiosity.

Suddenly, Isabel had a flash of insight. "Your mother..." she said. "Where is she now?"

Gabriel's mouth twisted in a grimace. "She died about three months ago."

"I'm so sorry," Isabel said automatically. She didn't know Gabriel, but she did know how hard it was to lose a parent. Wyatt rubbed her back gently, and she laid her hand on his thigh. He was no stranger to loss, either. His parents had abandoned him to the care of his grandfather when he was only three. Even though he'd had a happy childhood, she knew their rejection was a source of pain for him.

"Thank you."

"You have no one else?" Jose guessed.

"That's right," Gabriel confirmed.

"So you're just looking to belong?" Diego said. He put his hands on his hips, suspicious again.

"Partly," Gabriel said. He sounded a little evasive, which made Isabel frown.

"What do you want, son?" Jose said.

Gabriel blinked at his use of the familial term. Diego pressed his lips together in a thin line, clearly unhappy with his grandfather's acknowledgment of a blood connection, however informal.

"I want my share of the ranch." Gabriel's words hung in the air, small bombs destroying the fragile truce of a moment ago.

"Your share?" Diego was lethally quiet, his body practically emanating black waves. "What makes you think you have a share?"

Gabriel lifted his chin. "I'm a Cruz."

"Says you. We're supposed to take your word for it just because you show up here with an old check?" Diego nodded at Abuelo's desk. "For all I know, you forged that."

"I didn't—" Gabriel began, but Diego cut him off.

"Even if you are related, that doesn't mean squat."

Gabriel's thin smile lacked humor. "Is that what you think?"

A frisson of worry shot down Isabel's spine. If the look on his face was any indication, Gabriel knew something the rest of them didn't.

She glanced at Abuelo. He was staring into the distance, his attention a million miles away.

"What I think," Diego said, forcing the words from between his teeth, "is that the Cruz ranch belongs to those of us who work for it. I've been breaking my back on this land for the last twenty years. I don't remember seeing you out in the fields helping to round up cattle or taking care of the first morning feeds." He leaned forward, fists clenched at his sides. "If you think you can show up here with some crazy story and expect to be added to the business, you're even dumber than you look."

Gabriel ignored Diego, turning to look at Abuelo. "What do you say, Grandpa?" He placed a mocking emphasis on the last word, which set Isabel's teeth on edge.

Jose jumped, shaken out of his reverie. Isabel could see he wasn't prepared to respond, so she spoke up.

"You don't look like much of a cowboy to me," she observed. "Do you even know the first thing about ranching?"

Gabriel turned to face her, staring at her with the same dark brown eyes her father had had. "Well, that's the thing," he drawled. "I don't need to." He spread his hands out. "I'm a reasonable man. As you've deduced, I'm not much of a ranch hand. I'll be happy to take my share of the ranch as cash." He glanced at Diego. "You can buy me out, and I'll go away and never bother you again."

"I've got a better idea," Diego said, taking a menacing step forward. "You leave now and I'll let you walk out of here. If you come back, I'll consider it trespassing and defend this property and my family accordingly."

Isabel felt Wyatt tense beside her, clearly ready to jump up to his feet if either man made a move for the other.

Gabriel rose. Wyatt stood, as well, his expression alert. Gabriel gave him a mocking salute.

"I can see we're at an impasse for now. I'll give you all some time to consider my offer." He nodded at Abuelo, then glanced at Isabel and nodded again before moving toward the door.

Diego stepped in his path, blocking the way out. Alarm propelled Isabel out of the love seat, but she needn't have worried. Wyatt materialized at her brother's side, his hand on Diego's shoulder. His lips moved as he murmured something, but she couldn't tell what he was saying.

Gabriel and Diego eyed each other in silence. Gabriel had his back to her, but she could see Diego's face and knew her brother was simply looking for an excuse to do violence. *Please, don't give him one*, she pleaded silently.

Fortunately, Gabriel didn't take the bait. He waited patiently as Wyatt continued to speak in Diego's ear. Finally her brother stepped to the side, but not before shooting Gabriel a look that would have felled a weaker man.

If Gabriel was bothered by Diego's behavior, he didn't show it. He settled his hat on his head and touched the brim. "I'll see myself out," he said.

Diego turned on his heel as Gabriel left, clearly intent on following the other man. Wyatt held him back. "I'll go," he said. "I'll make sure he leaves."

Her brother hesitated then nodded. Wyatt walked

after Gabriel, his boot heels tapping out a fading cadence as he moved through the house.

Isabel sank back onto the cushion, her breath escaping in a gusty sigh. That had been…intense.

"Is this guy for real?" Diego moved to stand next to Abuelo's desk. He placed his hands on the worn wood surface and leaned forward, putting the older man in his shadow.

Jose looked miserable. "I think so," he said softly. He stared at the check on his desk. "I always wondered why it never cleared the bank. I'd assumed she'd lost it." He shook his head. "Now I know."

Diego shook his head. "I can't believe we're just going to take this guy at his word. Sure, he has the check, but how do we know Dad was really his father? Maybe his mother messed around with a lot of guys."

Isabel shot her brother a withering look. "Are you blind? He has Dad's eyes."

Her brother shrugged, clearly not convinced. "Lots of people have brown eyes. That doesn't mean anything."

"A DNA test will give you all the proof you need. If the two of you have the same Y chromosome, he's one of us." She didn't imagine Gabriel would be averse to providing a cheek swab. In fact, he'd probably welcome the chance to prove he was a Cruz, if only to further antagonize Diego.

"No," muttered Diego. "I don't care what the DNA says. He'll never be one of us."

Isabel looked at Abuelo. Gabriel had been strangely confident he was owed a part of the ranch, and her grandfather hadn't jumped in to contradict his assertion. What did the pair of them know that she didn't?

"Why does he think he's entitled to a share of the ranch?" she asked quietly. "Is there some stipulation we don't know about regarding how the land is passed down through the generations?"

"There is." Her grandfather sighed. "The ranch land and business is actually owned by a family trust. When it was created many years ago, the terms of the trust state that any Cruz family member can put forward a claim to a share of the property. Major decisions, such as selling the land or dissolving the business, require a unanimous agreement among all shareholders. But a person can choose to sell their portion of the business to another family member."

Wyatt slipped into the room and moved to sit next to her again. "He's gone," he said softly.

Diego cursed a blue streak. "Why are we just now hearing about this?" he demanded.

"Because until a few minutes ago, I thought the three of us were the only Cruz family members left," Abuelo said, a bite of temper in his voice. "My brothers are dead and they never married, so you don't have any cousins. And your father was my only child. As far as I knew, there was no need to go into the details of the family trust, since I didn't think it would affect you two in the short term."

Wyatt gave her a questioning look. Isabel shook her head and gave his knee a pat. *I'll fill you in later*, she promised silently.

"We have to get the terms of the trust changed," Diego declared. "Surely there's a way to do that?"

Abuelo shook his head. "It won't matter."

"Why not?" Diego challenged. "I find it hard to believe there's no way to amend the original terms of the trust."

"It requires a unanimous vote, doesn't it?" Isabel said.

Abuelo confirmed her suspicion with a nod. "And there's no way Gabriel will agree to a change that cuts him out of the deal."

"Why can't we change it now?" Diego asked. "He's not a confirmed Cruz—we could act before we have him take a DNA test."

"And then his lawyer will come after us and we'll have to shell out a boatload of money just to go back to the way things were originally," Isabel pointed out. Not for the first time, she wished her brother would use his head instead of letting his emotions rule.

"I will call the family attorney," Jose said. "He'll know what our options are."

"If any exist," Isabel said quietly. She didn't want to be a Negative Nancy, but Gabriel wasn't going to suddenly change his mind about staking his claim in this family. They were going to have to find a way to adjust to this news and its consequences. Given the fact that she and Diego were still at odds regarding the fracking offer, she didn't hold out much hope that adding another player to the mix would be an improvement.

"Can you afford to buy him out?" Wyatt gave voice to the question that had been circling through Isabel's mind for the last several minutes. Once a DNA test proved Gabriel was her half brother—which she figured was just a matter of time—he was entitled to his part of the ranch. Since he and Diego had gotten off to such an inauspicious start, it was probably for the best that they bought him out as he'd requested.

"No." Diego practically spat out the word. "Not the way things stand now. And I don't have nearly enough in my personal account for that."

"Me, neither," Isabel volunteered. She was still paying off vet school loans, and would be for the foreseeable future. It would be a long time before she accrued any kind of personal wealth, if she ever did.

"Then we're screwed."

"Language, *mijo.*"

They all turned at the sound of Maria's voice. She'd slipped into the room without anyone noticing. Now she walked over to Abuelo's desk and put her hand on his shoulder, looking down at him with concern. *"¿Como estas?"* she asked softly. *How are you?*

"Estare bien," said Abuelo. But his tired expression suggested he was anything but fine.

Maria pursed her lips. "Come into the kitchen. I've made some tea. It will help you think." She glanced at Diego. "You get to work. You need to burn off your anger." Finally, her eyes landed on Isabel. "And you need to rest. You look pale again."

No one argued. Diego sighed and walked out of the room without saying a word. Maria helped Abuelo stand and the pair of them headed for the door, leaving Wyatt and Isabel alone together for the first time since they were in her hospital room hours ago.

"Well…" He looked at her, clearly trying to process these recent revelations. "I'm not sure I know what to think about all of this."

Isabel snorted. "Welcome to the club."

He studied her face. "Are you all right? That was a lot of new information to process."

She smiled, touched by his concern. "It's okay. I kind of always suspected something was off between my parents, but I was too young to realize what it was. Once I grew up some, it didn't seem like it mattered since they were gone. It sucks to know my dad cheated on my mom, but I can't do anything to change that."

"You seem to be taking it a lot better than your brother."

Isabel tilted her head to the side. "I suppose. But in his defense, he had a different relationship with our dad. I remember him following Dad everywhere, dogging his heels like a small, determined shadow." Her heart ached a bit at the image of her brother tagging along with their father, staring up at him with a look of abject devotion on his young face. "It's going to take some time for him to process the fact that his hero was human, after all."

"Think he wants to talk about it?"

"Maybe?" She wasn't quite sure. Diego's mood was volatile at the moment. There was no way to know how he'd respond to Wyatt's offer of a friendly ear. "I'd give him some time to cool down first. But I think he would appreciate hearing that you've got his back."

"I've got yours, too. You know that, right?" He ran the pad of his thumb along her right cheekbone, sending a tingle dancing along her skin.

"I do," she confirmed. "But I might need you to keep telling me that." Between the family drama and yesterday's health scare, Isabel was feeling a little raw.

"Just say the word," Wyatt promised.

Isabel leaned toward him and rested her forehead on his shoulder. He slipped his arm around her and ran his hand down the valley of her spine in a soothing caress. She closed her eyes, soaking up his touch, breathing in his scent, wishing they could stay like this forever.

After a moment, Wyatt shifted. "Maria's right," he said, his voice quiet. "You still need rest. Let's get you to your room."

"What about you?"

"Me?" He looked confused.

"You didn't get any more sleep than I did last

night," she pointed out. "You've got to be tired, as well."

"Yeah, but—"

"No buts," Isabel said firmly, cutting off his protest. "Come upstairs with me. We can take a nap together."

"In your bed?" Wyatt looked shocked at the prospect. "Won't Maria and your grandfather have something to say about that?"

She laughed at his prim-and-proper response. "We're all adults here. Besides, they're not hypocrites."

Wyatt's eyes practically bugged out of his head. "You mean… The two of them…?" He whispered the last, turning to stare at the doorway and into the empty hall as though he was afraid the pair of them would reappear and catch them gossiping.

She nodded, enjoying his reaction. She'd picked up on the signs years ago, but it didn't surprise her to know the men in her life were less attuned to the interpersonal dynamics of the household. "Of course. What did you think?"

He shook his head. "To be honest, I didn't consider it. I generally don't spend a lot of time pondering the details of other people's sex lives."

"Can't say I blame you. And you're in good company. I'm not sure Diego knows about it."

"Really? Even though he lives here?" Wyatt sounded surprised at her brother's blinders, which struck her as funny given his own ignorance.

Isabel shrugged. "I'm sure on some level he suspects the two of them are more than friends, but denial is a powerful force." She got to her feet, held out her hand. "So what do you say? Ready to do something scandalous?"

Wyatt took her hand and stood, blue eyes twinkling as he stared down at her. "Lead the way."

Chapter 9

Wyatt woke slowly, emerging from the depths of sleep to float on the surface of consciousness on one long exhale.

He opened his eyes to find the room bathed in shades of gray. A glance at the window showed the sun was on its way down. Somehow, they'd managed to sleep away the afternoon.

Isabel stirred next to him. He watched her stretch, still half asleep as she shifted on the bed. There was something almost feline about the languid way she moved, her legs straightening, her arms reaching above her head as she slowly blinked awake.

She caught him watching, gave him a smile.

It was an invitation he couldn't pass up.

Wyatt leaned over and kissed her, unable to re-

sist the temptation any longer. He'd behaved himself
earlier when she'd brought him to her room. She'd
laid down on one side of the bed and he'd taken the
other half, and aside from a chaste peck on the cheek,
they hadn't touched. Looking back, he was surprised
at how quickly he'd fallen asleep. He'd thought his
proximity to Isabel would keep him awake, but his
lack of rest last night had taken its toll.

Now he felt refreshed and ready to pick up where
they'd left off on the bench outside the hospital that
morning.

Isabel's lips were soft against his own. She
hummed low in her throat and ran her hands through
his hair, holding his head in place to keep the kiss
going.

Wyatt was only too happy to oblige.

Zings of sensation zipped along his skin, leaving
goose bumps in their wake. They inched closer to
each other, their bodies closing the distance between
them until it was gone.

The first thing he registered was her warmth;
every point of contact between them felt like a live
coal. As he wrapped his arms around her, he felt
her body change against him. The languor of sleep
began to fade, replaced by a building tension in her
muscles. She was like a spring, coiling tighter and
tighter as the kiss deepened.

Desire nipped at the edges of his mind, a chorus
of need that grew stronger with each passing second until it threatened to drown out logical thought.

It was time to end the kiss. If they didn't stop now, he was going to have a hard time backing off later.

He pulled away reluctantly, putting space between them. The air was cold against his lips, an unwelcome sensation after the heat of Isabel's mouth.

She blinked at him, confusion plain in her eyes. "What's wrong?"

"Nothing." He knew he should stop touching her, but he reached out to push a strand of hair off her cheek. "I just figured we should pace ourselves."

"Is that what you want?"

No! his body cried. "Well…" he hedged. "Don't you want to take it slow?" He wasn't going to push her, or try to rush into resuming a physical relationship. He couldn't deny he felt a sense of urgency, a desire to make up for lost time now that they were both on the same page. But he didn't want to move too fast and risk spooking Isabel. He was interested in a long-term relationship with her, not a quick roll in the hay at the expense of an emotional connection.

A smile spread slowly across her face. "I don't, actually," she said. "I think we've been stuck in the slow lane for the last ten years. I'm ready to shift gears a bit." She lifted one leg and rolled on top of him, straddling his hips.

The blood drained out of Wyatt's head, rushing south to where Isabel sat upon him looking like a goddess with her dark hair flowing over her shoulders and down her back. "Are you okay with that?" she asked.

His body responded before he could say anything. She felt his arousal against her core and grinned slyly. "Should I take that as a yes?"

He nodded, reaching up for her. She leaned back a bit, evading his grasp. In one fluid motion, she hooked her thumbs under the hem of her shirt and pulled it up and over her head. Then she reached around and unhooked her bra, shrugging free of the straps.

Wyatt's mouth went dry as he stared up at her, hardly daring to believe this was happening. He didn't want to look away for fear that he'd glance back to find it was all a dream.

Isabel took his hands and brought them to her breasts. Her curves fit perfectly in his hands and the weight of them nearly pushed him over the edge.

She leaned forward, lowering her head to kiss him again. He slid his hands to her back, then down to her hips, gripping tightly so that she rocked against him. Isabel let out a small squeak when he flipped her over, reversing their positions so that he was on top.

Moving slowly, Wyatt lowered his weight onto her body. He was determined to savor every touch, every sensation. He'd lived off the memory of their first encounter for years, torturing himself with the thought he was never going to hold Isabel close again. But fortune had smiled on them and he was grateful for it. He wasn't going to take this time for granted.

They shed their remaining clothes and took turns exploring each other's body, getting reacquainted after so long apart. Their first time had been earnest but fumbling. Now they were both more experienced and more attuned to one another's needs. Every sigh, every soft gasp, told him she was enjoying herself, and her pleasure only served to heighten his own.

Eventually, Isabel stretched out her arm, reaching for the bedside table. Wyatt watched her pull open the drawer and fumble inside for a few seconds. She withdrew a small foil square and handed it to him.

"I can get back on the Pill," she said. "But for now, this will have to do."

"Whatever you prefer." His last health check had come back normal, but he knew they weren't ready for babies yet.

He could feel the heat from her gaze as she watched him slip on the condom. He'd always thought of birth control as a necessary precaution, but seeing Isabel lick her lips as she tracked his every move changed the experience from an extra step to something sexy.

Once the protection was in place, they came together again, touching everywhere. Isabel welcomed him into her body with a soft cry that was sweeter than any music.

The first time they'd slept together, Wyatt had lost a piece of his heart to Isabel. Over the last ten years, he'd wondered if his feelings that night had been real or just the hormonal flares of a young man.

Being with her now, he knew the magic between them went beyond the physical. This was a union not just of bodies but of hearts and souls, as well. Isabel was the only woman for him, the only person he'd ever connected with so fully.

She tensed under him, her breath catching. Her body shuddered as she let out a sigh of satisfaction, her core gripping him tightly.

The added sensation sent Wyatt over the edge. He thrust again then dropped his head to nuzzle her neck. Her warm scent filled his lungs as his body emptied, a combination that left him dizzy.

After an endless moment, Wyatt moved to the side so he wouldn't crush Isabel with his weight. She let out a soft sound of protest at the change in position. He hooked his arm around her waist and drew her close, tucking her against his chest. He tugged the sheets over their bodies to ward off the chill of the room.

"Wow." She sounded dazed and a little breathless.

A swell of masculine satisfaction pulsed through him, making him feel ten feet tall.

"Yeah." He kissed her shoulder.

"So the first time wasn't a fluke." There was a note of wonder in her voice, as though she couldn't quite believe it.

Wyatt laughed, amazed at how in sync their thoughts had been. "Definitely not."

She rolled to face him, her brown eyes bright with mischief. "What about the third time? How do you think that will go?"

A wave of heat rolled through him. He leaned forward and nipped at her bottom lip.

"Give me a few minutes and we'll find out."

It was well past the dinner hour by the time Isabel and Wyatt left her room to sneak downstairs for a snack. They'd spent the last several hours making love and talking, tucked away in the sanctuary of her room. With the door closed and the curtains drawn, it had been easy to pretend like they were the only two people in the world. All the stresses of the past several days had receded as they had focused on each other.

It would have been nice to stay in her room forever, loving and chatting and sleeping. But their stomachs weren't on board with that plan and eventually their hunger pangs grew too intense to ignore much longer.

Isabel felt like the rebellious teenager she'd never been as she and Wyatt descended the stairs. She was careful to step lightly so as not to wake Abuelo. There was no chance he and Maria were unaware that Wyatt was still in the house, and they likely had no illusions as to what Isabel had been doing this afternoon. Still, discretion was always in style, at least in Isabel's mind.

"Do you think Maria will get mad at us for rummaging in her kitchen?" Wyatt whispered behind her.

"Not if we clean up after ourselves," Isabel whispered back.

There was a faint glow coming from the room; Maria must have left the light on over the stove, knowing they'd need to eat at some point. Isabel smiled, but her lips froze as she stepped into the kitchen and saw it wasn't empty.

Diego sat at the table, chewing on a sandwich and staring into the distance.

He glanced up as they walked in. His gaze flicked from Isabel to Wyatt and then back again. Anxiety was a sour taste in her mouth as she braced for her brother's reaction.

To her great shock, Diego didn't say anything. He merely nodded at them both and took another bite of his sandwich.

It was Wyatt who broke the silence.

"Hey, man," he said. "You doing okay?"

Diego swallowed, took a sip from the beer bottle in front of him. "Who's asking?" He tilted his head to the side, studying Wyatt. "My friend, or my sister's boyfriend?"

Isabel flinched. *You ass.*

She opened her mouth to respond, angry on Wyatt's behalf. But his hand on her shoulder stopped her.

"Can't I be both?" Wyatt asked. "There's enough of me to go around." His tone was light but Isabel heard the note of strain in his voice.

Diego finished his beer and rose, carrying the empty plate and bottle to the sink. Isabel stepped aside to let her brother pass as he approached, but Wyatt didn't move.

The two men stood facing each other for a moment, the silence between them growing thick with everything they weren't saying. After what seemed like an eternity, Diego spoke.

"Night, y'all."

With that, he sidestepped Wyatt and headed down the hall.

Wyatt stared after him, his expression bewildered. Isabel touched his arm and he turned to look at her.

"Do you want to go after him?" It was clear the two of them needed to talk.

Wyatt frowned then shook his head. "He's not in any mood to listen right now." He smiled at her, but it was strained. "Let's get something to eat."

She followed him deeper into the kitchen, her thoughts whirling as she collected the ingredients for sandwiches. The last thing she wanted was to come between Diego and his best friend. But... Wyatt had her heart. As much as she hated to admit it, she wasn't going to let him go without a fight.

Even if that meant she had to battle her own brother.

On the heels of that thought came another realization; she wasn't the only one in this relationship. What did Wyatt think? Would he go along with Diego's game and make a choice between them, which was what her brother seemed to want?

And what if he didn't pick her?

She frowned, indignation filling her as she played the scenario out in her mind. It was possible Wyatt might decide his friendship with Diego was more important than their developing relationship. After all, they'd had a chance ten years ago and it hadn't worked out. And they hadn't reconciled their differing opinions on the drilling proposal, which was still a point of contention. Would he want to let go of his best friend to take a shot on her when their track record was so spotty?

"Penny for your thoughts."

His voice broke into her reverie, bringing her back to the present. "What?"

Wyatt gestured to her hands. "You've been spreading peanut butter on that slice of bread for the last few minutes. I don't think it needs any more."

She looked down to find he was correct. Feeling flustered, she shoved the knife into the jar and reached for another slice. "Sorry," she muttered.

"It's all the same to me," he said. "I love peanut butter. The more the better."

When she didn't respond, he reached for her hand. "Are you going to tell me what's bothering you?"

"I'm fine," she replied automatically. In truth, she wasn't sure how she felt—her thoughts were too disorganized, her emotions too disjointed. How could she be expected to think rationally about their relationship when her muscles still twinged from their earlier encounters?

"Isabel." She glanced up to find Wyatt watching her, his blue eyes knowing. "I'm not going to dump you to appease your brother."

Her jaw dropped as she stared at him. "How did you...?" Was the man psychic?

He smiled. "You're thinking very loudly," he said. "And you have a terrible poker face."

She snorted. "It's not *that* bad."

"Hey." He stepped over to her and drew her close, wrapping his arms around her and resting his chin on the top of her head. She placed her ear flat against his chest, directly over the steady thump of his heart.

His voice vibrated against her as he spoke. "I care about you. A lot. I want to see what happens between us. I'm not going to let your brother get in the way of that."

"But what about the drilling? Despite my theories on the cyanide, I still think we should consider that company's offer. It could have been a rogue worker, if they were involved at all." Would he be able to overlook her pragmatism, especially since it flew in the face of his life's work?

He shrugged. "I don't agree with your stance, that's true. It's not enough to make me want to walk away, though."

It was exactly what she needed to hear. Her body relaxed against him as some of the stiffness left her muscles. "But what about Diego? You guys have been friends for ages. I don't want you to lose that." And it wasn't just Wyatt she worried about; Diego didn't have a large collection of friends. If he and Wyatt parted ways, who would her brother turn to then?

"I won't." He sounded supremely confident. Isabel wished she shared his optimism.

"How do you know?"

"Because I'll get him to see there is no choice here. He and I can stay friends, and you and I can be…something more." He punctuated the last with a subtle thrust of his hips that left no room for doubt as to his meaning.

Warmth blossomed low in her belly. "That sounds nice," she said softly. He made it seem so simple. If only that were really the case…

"Stop worrying," he commanded.

She pulled back and looked up at him. "How did you know?" He hadn't been able to see her face, so her expression couldn't have given her away.

He smiled and dropped a kiss on the tip of her nose. "I can feel you getting tense." He placed his hands on her shoulders and kneaded gently. "Come on, let's finish making those sandwiches. It's easier to think on a full stomach."

"I suppose that's true," she said. He released her and they turned back to the counter.

"Please don't worry, Isabel," he said. "This is between me and Diego. We'll work it out."

"I'll try," she said. "But I can't make any promises."

His mouth tilted in a half smile. "I guess I'll just have to keep you distracted."

"Promise?"

He kissed her again, this time on the mouth. When

he pulled away a moment later, Isabel's skin was flushed and she was no longer thinking about her brother. Or anything else, for that matter.

"Promise."

Chapter 10

"Do you have to go?" Isabel stood in the barn, watching Wyatt as he saddled Ajax. Dust motes and bits of horsehair drifted in the morning light, but she only had eyes for Wyatt.

They'd slept in each other's arms last night and it had been the best rest she'd had in years. He'd woken early with her to help her check the cows—none were in labor yet, but it was just a matter of time.

Maria had cooked a large breakfast and, while she hadn't directly commented on the turn in their relationship, her frequent smiles and knowing looks made it clear she approved. Even Abuelo had given them his blessing, shuffling over to the table to lay one hand on Isabel's shoulder and the other on Wyatt's. He'd squeezed gently, nodded once and taken his place at the head of the table.

Isabel appreciated the gestures of support. Even though she didn't require her family's permission, it meant a lot to know they approved of Wyatt.

Diego had been missing from the breakfast table, but she still held out hope he would come around. Her brother wasn't known for a cooperative spirit, but Isabel trusted Wyatt's judgment that eventually Diego would see there was no need to make things difficult.

Maria agreed. "You know your brother," she'd said, patting Wyatt on the shoulder as she'd moved behind him. "He always has to take the long way around to a conclusion."

Their bellies full, Isabel and Wyatt had helped clean the kitchen. Now, having run out of delaying tactics, it was time for him to go, and she waited for his answer to her question about his need to leave.

He glanced over, his blue eyes shiny with longing. "You know I do."

"Yeah." She exhaled and leaned over the stall door. "I just wish you didn't."

"Me, too." He bent over, lifted one of Ajax's feet and inspected the hoof. "I'll ask for more time off later. But I need to get back to real life, and you do, too."

She knew he was right, but the idea of falling back into her usual routine was unappealing. Now that she and Wyatt had reconnected, she wanted to spend all her time with him. Ten years apart added up to a lot of missed moments and she had every intention of making them up.

"Besides," Wyatt continued, moving on to check another foot, "I think Diego will cool down faster if I'm not always here."

A sudden spurt of anger made Isabel push off the stall door. "I don't care," she declared hotly. "He can grow up and deal with his emotions like an adult, the way the rest of us do. I'm not going to cast my own happiness aside just because he's acting like a spoiled child."

Wyatt released Ajax's leg and straightened. "I'm not suggesting that," he said mildly. "But it's only been two days. We need to figure out a routine that works for us. You and me," he added hastily, seeing her brows rise. "As much as I want to spend every minute with you, I have to work. So do you. We'll come up with a schedule that accommodates us both."

Isabel knew he was right. She knew it was unreasonable to think they'd be inseparable from here on out. But her heart wanted what it wanted and it wasn't interested in listening to reason.

"What time will you be off work tonight?" she said. "Maybe I can come to you this time?" She knew he lived at a campsite for park employees, but she'd never had occasion to go there.

He finished checking the horse's hooves and walked to the stall door. "That would be nice. We still have to come up with a plan for the ranch that doesn't involve drilling. I want to help with that." He reached up to brush a strand of hair behind her ear. "Do you know where to find me?"

She nodded. "Panther Junction, right?"

"That's the place." He gave her directions to his cabin. "How about six tonight? I should be home by then."

"All right." Knowing she was going to see him again in a few hours made it a little easier to say goodbye now.

She unlatched the door and stepped aside to allow Wyatt to lead Ajax out of the stall. The horse gave her a friendly sniff as he walked past.

"Is it my imagination or has he put on a little weight in the past two days?" Now that they were out of the barn, she could see Ajax's whole body in the sun. He was a beautiful animal, powerfully built but still graceful. *Much like his rider*, she mused.

Wyatt smacked the horse's rump affectionately. "He's had it easy, hanging out with Miel and eating his fill of hay. Ruben said they put him out to pasture yesterday, but that's not enough exercise for this boy."

"How are you getting back to the park?"

Wyatt reached into his pocket. "Your grandfather told me about a gate in the fence a few miles out. He gave me this, told me to keep it." He pulled out a small key, shiny in the morning light.

Isabel nodded, pleased to see it. "If Abuelo told you to keep it, then he trusts you."

Wyatt smiled broadly. "I know. It means a lot to me."

"You're as good as family now."

His smile turned sly. "But still adopted, right? Because otherwise, this would be weird." He pulled her close, dropping his head to kiss her.

Isabel gripped his shoulders, kissing him back for all she was worth. He tasted of sweet coffee and a subtle spice that was his alone. The potent combination made her head spin. What was it about this man that was so intoxicating? He had only to look at her and the world around them disappeared.

All too soon, the kiss was over. "Well," he said, a little breathless. "Remind me not to make that mistake again. I can't remember why I need to leave when you respond like that."

Isabel laughed and placed her palm on his chest. "Just trying to give you something to remember me by." She swiped her thumb across his nipple in a teasing stroke that made him suck in a breath.

"There's no chance of me forgetting you," he growled. He held her gaze for a moment then turned away with a shudder of effort. "No more distractions," he said, though she wasn't sure if he was talking to himself or to her.

He climbed up into the saddle easily, gathering the reins in one hand. "Tonight," he said, staring down at her.

She nodded, a silent promise.

With a final smile, he looked up and nudged Ajax into a walk. But just as soon as the horse began to move, Wyatt pulled back on the reins.

"You've got to be kidding me." He cursed, shaking his head in disgust.

Isabel turned around, wondering what had caused such a sudden change in his mood. Then she let out her own string of profanity.

Two vehicles were driving up the private ranch road, a cloud of dust trailing behind them. Gabriel's truck was in the lead, followed by a gray truck with a decal on the door. Even from this distance, she recognized the logo for the Praline Energy Corporation.

"Great," she muttered. Just what they needed today—a clutch of unwelcome visitors.

She glanced back at Wyatt. She hated to keep him from his work much longer, but it would be nice to have his help.

"Do you think—"

He swung his leg over Ajax's back before she could even finish the question. "Of course I'll stay," he said. "Give me a hand?"

They returned to the barn where she helped him remove the saddle and bridle from his horse. He slipped a lead over Ajax's head. "Let's turn him out here," she suggested, guiding the pair toward a nearby pasture. Ajax waited patiently as they opened the gate and then entered with a friendly nicker to the other animals inside.

"All right," Wyatt said. "Let's do this."

They walked over to the house, arriving just as Gabriel and the second truck pulled up. Isabel took Wyatt's hand and climbed the porch steps to stand by the door. It was a small thing, but she wanted to be taller than these men, if only for a moment.

Gabriel climbed out, did another slow survey of the house and the nearby pastures.

"You're back," Wyatt said, his tone easy.

Gabriel nodded. "Good to see you again. Sister," he added, with a small smirk.

Isabel pressed her lips together but didn't reply.

The men from the energy company approached the porch. "Ms. Cruz. Is your grandfather available? Or perhaps your brother?"

She stepped forward. "It's Dr. Cruz," she said icily. "And no, they're not free at the moment. What do you need?"

"Actually, I'm right here," Gabriel said.

The man looked surprised. "Oh, I don't believe we've met. I'm Robert Anderson. This is my associate Gavin Brewster." The men all shook hands.

"Gabriel Richardson Cruz," he replied smoothly. "The long-lost brother."

Isabel's anger built as she watched the three of them talk, these self-appointed masters of the universe who thought they could come onto her family's property and discuss its future as though she wasn't even there.

Gabriel's expression turned calculating when he

heard about the energy company's attempt to buy the ranch's mineral rights.

Great, she thought to herself. *Now he'll be even more insufferable.*

"Excuse me." When they continued talking, she cleared her throat and tried again, louder this time.

All three of them turned to look at her. "None of you are welcome here. You." She pointed to Gabriel. "You have not yet proven your connection to this family. I'd advise you not to insert yourself into Cruz family business until you are legally able to do so." She turned to the energy company representatives next. "And as for you gentlemen, we will be in touch when we have made a decision."

"Ms. Cruz," said Robert, stepping forward. "Uh, Dr. Cruz," he hastily amended after a glance at her face. "We're here because the terms of the offer have changed. We were hoping to discuss them with you all."

Of course, she thought sourly. It was just as she'd feared—they were going to rescind their offer. But as much as she'd like to discuss it with them, she wasn't in the habit of conducting business on the porch.

And certainly not in front of strangers.

"It seems you've wasted a trip," she said. Maybe, by stalling, she could convince her grandfather and brother to make a counterproposal so they could still get some money. "Next time, pick up the phone and make an appointment."

Robert and Gavin exchanged a look. "Well, ma'am,

that's the thing," said Gavin. "We're required to provide you with a written copy of the new offer and to make sure you understand the new terms." He held up a manila folder.

Isabel marched over and took it from him. "We'll look over the paperwork and call if we have any questions."

"But, Miss—"

"Goodbye," she said firmly.

When they hesitated, Wyatt moved behind her. "Gentlemen," he said, his voice low. "You've been dismissed."

After an awkward pause, the pair walked back to their truck. A few seconds later they were driving away, their tires kicking up dust.

Isabel eyed Gabriel, who hadn't moved. "That goodbye applies to you, as well."

"Don't be so uptight, sis." He stepped forward.

Wyatt appeared at her side, making Gabriel pause. "The lady asked you to leave."

Gabriel tilted his head back to take Wyatt's measure. "Who are you, exactly? And what's your connection to the family?"

Isabel spoke before Wyatt could respond. "That's not your concern." She certainly wasn't going to explain anything to Gabriel, nor did she appreciate his assumption that he had a right to that information.

Gabriel gave Wyatt one last look before turning to Isabel. "I need to speak to Jose. Where is he?"

"As I said before," she replied, tightening her grip on her temper, "he's not available. Leave a message."

Gabriel snorted in disgust. "Fine, have it your way," he muttered. "Here." He pulled a folded sheaf of papers from his back pocket and thrust them forward. "From my attorney."

"Oh?" She glanced at them, but she didn't have enough experience with legalese to immediately understand what they said.

"It's a court order," he explained. "Preventing you all from making changes to the structure of the Cruz family trust until the details of my relationship to the family are established." She glanced up in surprise, and he gave her a thin smile. "Just in case you thought you could cut me out before I prove I'm a Cruz."

"We weren't going to try."

He laughed. "Sure. You might think that way, but I know Diego is racking his brain to come up with a way to get rid of me. And now that I know my share is worth more than I initially thought, I can't say that I blame him."

"I could always shoot you." Diego strolled onto the porch, a shotgun in one hand and a bag in the other. The barrel was pointed to the ground, but Isabel tensed instinctively. Once again, her brother had decided to overreact.

Gabriel shifted, his eyes never leaving the gun. "Is that right?" He sounded a little uneasy, as though he thought Diego was just crazy enough to do it.

At least he's not a total idiot, Isabel thought. *He knows better than to poke the bear.*

"Oh, yeah." Diego nodded. "The way I see it,

we've got a lot of land out here." He paused, stared at Gabriel. "A lot," he repeated for emphasis. "And seeing as how you're all alone in the world, I doubt anyone would miss you."

Isabel tried not to roll her eyes at her brother's theatrics. Diego was hotheaded, but he wasn't a murderer.

Keeping his eyes on Gabriel, Diego disassembled the gun and began to clean the barrel.

"That's the thing, though," Gabriel said.

Isabel couldn't help but notice that he'd waited to respond until he was in no danger of being shot.

"I'm not alone," he continued. "Like it or not, I'm one of you. And I'm ready to take a DNA test to prove it. I'd hoped to talk to Jose about that, but a sample from you would work just as well."

"I'm busy."

"It doesn't have to be now," Gabriel said.

"I'll be busy for a while."

Wyatt made a soft sound of amusement and Isabel bit her lip to keep from smiling. Mule-headed was too weak a term for her brother.

"I'll do it." Abuelo stood just inside the house, his face obscured by the screen door. "What do you need?"

A look of relief crossed Gabriel's face. "Just a cheek swab."

"Fine." Abuelo stepped onto the porch and cast a dark look at Diego, who was now reassembling the rifle. "Where do we go?"

"There's a place in Alpine," Gabriel said. "I might

be able to have them send someone out here, so you don't have to make the trip."

"No, I will go," said Abuelo. He turned to Isabel. "Drive me, please?"

"Of course." She glanced at Gabriel. "Where is it?"

He tapped on his phone for a minute then turned the screen to face her. "Just here. You can follow me there." Now that he was no longer facing off with Diego, he was a lot more pleasant.

She glanced at her grandfather, who nodded. "Give us a few minutes," she said. She took a step toward the house, but before she reached the door the walkie-talkie on Diego's hip squawked to life.

"Diego, come in." It was Ruben, and he sounded flustered.

"I'm here. What's going on?"

"I found more cyanide traps," he said, his tone grim.

Isabel's heart dropped. Behind her, Wyatt sucked in a breath.

"Don't touch them!" Diego commanded. "Just stay put. I'm coming to you."

Ruben rattled off his location. "Bring the truck," he said grimly. "We've lost several more animals."

"You don't have to do this." Isabel glanced at him then went back to tightening the straps on Miel's saddle.

"The hell I don't," Wyatt replied roughly. "I don't

want you anywhere near those traps. If you're going, so am I."

She lifted her foot and placed it in one stirrup then climbed on top of the horse. "Just out of curiosity," she said, regarding him from her now lofty height. "What are you going to do? Throw yourself on top of the trap to keep me safe?"

"If that's what it takes," he grumbled. He mounted Ajax and now it was his turn to look down at her. "Everyone out there is going to be worried about the cattle. Someone's got to be focused on you."

Her eyes softened. "I'll be fine," she said.

"I know," he replied. "Because I'll be there to make sure of it."

"But what about your job? I don't want you to get in trouble because you're not back in the park yet."

He waved away her objection. "Let me worry about that. I already radioed in. They understand." And even if they hadn't given him the go-ahead for more time off? He'd still be right there, making sure she was safe.

She didn't look convinced.

"I'm not leaving you," he said firmly. "You seem to have forgotten that you were lying in a hospital bed a mere twenty-four hours ago. And while you might be feeling fine now, your doctors did tell you to take it easy for the next few days. I doubt riding several miles on horseback in the heat to examine animals who likely died from cyanide poisoning qualifies as rest."

Isabel gave him a mock glare. "You're as bad as Maria," she muttered. But he saw the smile she tried to hide as she turned away.

"And you're as stubborn as your grandfather." The old man had insisted on driving out to the site with Diego, and no amount of argument had been able to persuade him to stay home.

This time, she didn't try to hide her smile. "Guilty as charged." She nudged Miel into a walk and Wyatt followed suit. "They've made it work for years. Maybe that's a good sign for us?"

His heart flip-flopped at the note of hope in her voice. "I'd like to think so."

It didn't take long to reach the site of the problem. Diego and Jose were already there, the former helping the latter manage on the uneven ground. Ruben stood a few feet away, hands on hips as he stared at the ground.

"How many?" Isabel slid to the ground and started for Ruben, intent on seeing the damage firsthand. Wyatt quickly dismounted and hurried after her; she was so focused on Ruben she wasn't paying attention to the ground. She could step on or trip over another trap. The last thing she needed was another exposure of cyanide. She'd gotten lucky last time. She might not do as well after a second dose.

He caught up to her in a few strides. He scanned the ground as they walked toward Ruben, but he saw no signs of a trap. Still, he wasn't about to relax.

Ruben approached, holding his hands up as he

tried to stop Isabel. "There's nothing you can do," he said. "Don't go getting in the middle of them—I'm not sure how many traps there are yet."

She stopped, craning her neck to peer past his shoulder. Then she let out a soft cry that hit Wyatt like a slap. "Oh my God."

He turned to look, knowing it must be bad. But he still felt a jolt as he surveyed the scene.

Five, six, he counted silently. No...ten.

It was a large number of animals. And worse still, Wyatt could tell by the rounded bellies that most of the cows had been pregnant.

Isabel stayed rooted to the spot, her eyes shiny with tears as she stared at the gruesome sight. Diego and Jose walked over to join them and, for a moment, there was silence as each person tried to process what had happened.

"Where's the trap?" Diego's voice was flat, as if he'd been drained of all emotion.

"Over here," Ruben said, nodding to a spot in the middle of the bodies.

"Show me." He passed Jose's hand over to Isabel, who took it with a nod. Wyatt gave her a questioning look. She nodded again and he started off after Diego and Ruben.

He noticed the hay first. A trail of it leading to a larger pile, just like before. They stayed a good distance away from the spot, but from what he could see, it looked like the same kind of device that he and Isabel had found.

"Think this one has been modified, as well?"

Ruben gave him a sharp look. "Modified?"

Diego nodded. "Someone altered the last one so it would fire more easily."

"Huh," Ruben remarked. "I don't know about this one. I didn't get close enough to really inspect it."

"There's got to be more out here."

"What makes you say that?" Diego asked.

Wyatt looked around. The bodies didn't appear to be in any particular order, but there did seem to be a second concentration of them off to the left. "There are too many animals here. Even with modifications, I'd expect one trap to kill a few cows. But ten? That takes a lot of cyanide."

"He's right," Diego said, eyes scanning the ground. "I wonder how many more are out here."

"Look for the hay," Wyatt suggested. "That seems to be what the saboteur is using to draw them in."

A few yards away he found a dusting of hay that led back to a second larger pile. "Here," he said, pointing.

"And here," came Diego's voice from somewhere behind him.

Three in one spot. Talk about escalation.

He turned to find Isabel. She was still standing at the periphery of the site, supporting her grandfather. Jose was clinging to her arm, clearly distraught over the loss of animals.

Diego walked over to his sister and Wyatt joined them. "Why don't you head back to the house?" He pulled the keys to the truck from his pocket and handed them to her. "You can't help them now and Abuelo needs to get out of the sun."

"I should take samples," she said, but Diego shook his head.

"No need. We know what happened here."

"What are you going to do?" Jose's voice was weak, but he held his head high.

"Dig up the traps. Deal with the carcasses."

"Won't you need the truck?"

"No." Diego looked at Wyatt and then Ruben. "It would take too many trips back and forth to haul them in. We'll establish a perimeter, do a controlled burn."

"Are you sure that's a good idea?" Isabel glanced at Wyatt, the worry plain in her eyes.

He gave her a reassuring nod. "It'll be fine," he said. "There's no wind today. As long as we set it up right, we'll be okay."

"Why don't you just let the sheriff's department deal with the traps?" she suggested.

It was clear she didn't like the thought of any of them disturbing the devices and, after her experiences, Wyatt didn't blame her.

Diego stepped close and drew her into a hug. "Don't fret, sis. I've got this."

Isabel met Wyatt's eyes over her brother's shoulder. He gave her a small smile and a nod, trying to offer reassurance. "I'll take care of him," he promised, slapping Diego on the back.

"And who will take care of you?" she asked.

"I will." They both turned to look at Diego.

"Oh, come on," he said. "Don't look so surprised. I'd never let anything happen to you."

"So we're friends again?" Wyatt wasn't sure how far he could push Diego, but he was curious to know what the other man was thinking.

"Always." Diego slid a glance toward his sister. "And I guess you belong to her, too."

Isabel smiled broadly. "That he does. You're both mine, and I want you both to stay safe."

"We will," they said in unison. They all smiled, but the moment of levity was short-lived.

"Who is doing this to us?" asked Jose. "And why?"

Diego frowned, all traces of humor gone from his face. "I don't know, Abuelo. But we're going to find out."

Chapter 11

"Thank you, *mija*." Abuelo's voice was low, barely audible over the rumble of the truck's engine as they sped along the highway.

Isabel reached out and took his weathered hand in her own. "No thanks necessary. I'm happy to help."

They were headed home now, on the way back from Alpine. After leaving Diego, Ruben and Wyatt to deal with the dead animals and the cyanide traps, Abuelo had insisted on going to Alpine instead of to the ranch house.

"I want to take the DNA test now," he'd said stubbornly. Recognizing the futility of protest, Isabel had made a quick stop at the ranch house and then set off again, delivering him to the testing lab in Alpine. Gabriel was long gone, but fortunately, Isabel had remembered the name of the company she'd seen on his phone screen. A quick search of her own had pulled up the address. The whole procedure had taken surprisingly little time. They'd filled out paperwork, paid a small fee, and then a smiling woman in blue scrubs had taken a few cheek swabs from Abuelo's mouth.

"How long will this take?" he'd asked.

The woman lifted one shoulder as she sealed everything up and made sure the labels were correct. "Not long. We already have Mr. Richardson's sample, and it's a fairly straightforward process. You paid for expedited service, so I estimate we'll have an answer for you tomorrow afternoon."

"Excellent."

Isabel had asked her grandfather if there was anything else he wanted to do in Alpine. They usually made the drive about once a month for supplies, so an extra trip into town was a bit of a treat.

He'd looked around, his eyes listless as he'd taken in the shops and cafés that lined the street. "No," he'd said finally. "Let's just go home."

Isabel pressed a little harder on the accelerator, her thoughts focused on Wyatt and the mess he was helping to clean up. Were they almost done? Was he being safe? Hopefully no one had been hurt while dealing with the traps. Cell phone service out here was spotty at best, so if someone had been exposed to cyanide, it would take time for help to arrive.

She knew she'd gotten lucky the other day—she'd

stumbled upon a single trap that had already fired, leaving behind only residue instead of a high concentration of toxin. Even so, that had been enough to put her in the hospital. Now the men were dealing with three traps, which meant three chances for disaster to strike. What if they hadn't all been triggered? What if there was still a full dose of cyanide remaining in one of the traps, waiting to fire? Her brain conjured up a vision of Wyatt's limp body in the dirt, his lips blue as he desperately gasped for air.

She shook her head, trying to dismiss the disturbing image. But her heart still pounded with worry.

"They are fine." Abuelo patted her hand. "Try to relax."

She didn't bother to ask how he knew what she was thinking. "I hope you're right."

"I am. Your brother is impulsive, but he knows when to be careful. He will not take unnecessary risks."

"Who is doing this to us?" She knew she sounded plaintive, but she'd spent most of her life looking to Abuelo for advice and reassurance. It was a hard habit to break.

"I do not know." He was quiet for a moment, his mood pensive. "I have tried to live my life without hurting anyone. It seems that I have failed."

"No." She couldn't stand to have Abuelo think that any of this was his fault. He was a kind man, a decent human being who had showed her nothing but love her whole life. How could anyone want to go after him like this? "You are not to blame here."

"I wish I shared your confidence," he said. "But it feels like whoever is setting these traps is trying to settle some kind of score."

Isabel was beginning to suspect the same thing. The first trap had taken out three animals. Now they were dealing with three traps and ten dead cattle. Would there be another incident? Or did their faceless tormentor have something else in mind?

"What about Diego?" It was a possibility they'd discussed when she'd been in the hospital. "I've always known his bark is worse than his bite, but do you think he angered the wrong person?"

Abuelo sighed. "I've asked him that very question. He said he can't think of anyone who might want to target the ranch in this way. I believe him." She saw him shrug from the corner of her eye. "Diego tends to settle his disagreements quickly, sometimes with fists. It's not the best way to handle problems, but it does seem to be effective. He doesn't hold grudges, or nurse hurt feelings so they fester into something worse."

"But do all his friends feel the same way?" It was one thing for Diego to forgive and forget quickly. Not everyone embraced that philosophy.

Abuelo shook his head. "Who can say?"

"I doubt Maria has any enemies," Isabel said.

That earned her a laugh. "Of course not. No one would dare to cross her."

"So that leaves me." A stone of worry formed in her stomach as the implications sank in. She'd never thought of herself as the type of person to have adversaries. There were people she didn't like, certainly, but she'd never had the kind of interaction that left her filled with hate, and she certainly didn't think she'd triggered that kind of emotion in anyone else.

"I find it unlikely you could have done anything to cause this."

She wanted to think her grandfather was right. But someone in the family had inspired these attacks. It pained her to think that one of her relatives was the object of such hate, but what other explanation was there? They hadn't been picked at random. There was a reason her family and the ranch were being targeted in this way.

And she had a sinking suspicion that, until they figured out what it was, the hits would keep coming.

It was almost dark by the time Wyatt and Diego returned to the big house. He was tired down to his bones, but before he could go inside and collapse into Isabel's arms, he needed to see to Ajax. The horse had done well today; they'd used him, Miel and Ruben's mount to help position the carcasses of the dead cattle into a pile that they'd then set on fire. Ajax wasn't trained as a ranch horse, but he'd been amazingly cooperative. It was as though he could sense the prevailing mood of frustration and anger, and was trying to help as best he could.

He and Diego led the horses into the far end of the stable; Ruben's horse occupied a stall closer to the entrance. Wyatt removed the bridles and secured both mounts to loops on the wall while Diego filled two large buckets with water and placed one in front of each animal. While the horses drank, they removed the saddles and tack.

Wyatt grabbed two currycombs and passed one to Diego. There was something soothing about the repetitive motion of brushing Ajax, and he knew from experience his mount enjoyed this evening ritual very much.

"She's doing better." He nodded at Miel, who had her nose in the water bucket. "When I met her a couple of days ago, she was still shying around the scent of blood." She'd balked a few times today, but Diego's patient coaxing had helped her overcome her worry.

"Yeah." Diego gave her an affectionate pat as he moved down her side with the comb. "We'll make a cattle horse out of her yet."

Wyatt was quiet a moment, letting the events of the day wash over him as he moved on autopilot. The three M44 traps they'd pulled from the ground all bore the same modifications as the one that Isabel had discovered. They'd all been baited the same way, too, with small piles of hay piled on top to attract the grazing cows.

Ten animals. He shook his head at the waste of it. Ten otherwise healthy cattle; more, if you considered the calves that had been days away from birth. Wyatt wasn't certain how big the Cruz herd was, but a loss like this would likely have a large impact on their bottom line.

But while the financial implications of this loss were disturbing, Wyatt was more bothered by the fact that whoever was responsible for this sabotage was escalating.

"This isn't going to stop." He pitched his voice low, wanting to keep this conversation between the two of them.

Diego let out a heavy sigh. "I know." He was silent a moment. "I just wish I knew why it was happening."

Wyatt finished brushing one side of Ajax and circled around to the other, putting him closer to Diego. "Does it matter?"

Diego opened his mouth but Wyatt continued before he could speak. "I know it matters in the larger scheme of things. Of course, the motive is important. But worrying about why it's happening isn't going to get us any closer to figuring out who is doing it and how they're getting away with it."

"They're getting away with it because we have no way of monitoring every inch of our land." Diego sounded frustrated. Miel shifted and his face softened. He eased up on the pressure of the comb and she settled down again. "I'd love to upgrade the perimeter fencing, but we don't have the funds. The few cameras we do have don't cover enough of the property. And we're too far away from the border with Mexico for the Border Patrol to care about monitoring traffic out here."

He shook his head. "Isabel is pushing for us to downsize as much as we can, but Abuelo is fighting her at every turn. He thinks we're giving up. I'm trying to make him see we need to shrink so that we can keep the ranch going—she and I do agree on that point. That's why she's so gung-ho about the offer from the energy company." He bent at the waist and began to rub Miel's lower legs with a towel. "Those funds would be a real shot in the arm for us. But I just can't help but think we'd be trading short-term benefits for long-term problems."

"Why do you do it?" Wyatt asked. He exchanged the currycomb for a stiff brush and began to flick the dirt off Ajax's hide. Diego was painting a bleak picture of the challenges the ranch faced. "You don't have to be a rancher," he said. "Once upon a time, you wanted to coach baseball."

Diego huffed out a laugh. "Yeah." He straightened, shrugged. "Times change. The more I got involved with the business of the ranch, the more it appealed to me. And it's tradition, after all."

"You can't separate the ranch from your family, can you?"

His friend glanced at him, eyes flaring wide with surprise. It was all the confirmation Wyatt needed that his remark had hit home.

They worked in silence for a few minutes. Wyatt

had no words to offer Diego. For the first time, he realized his friend might be giving up more than he let on to keep the ranch alive. Sympathy welled in Wyatt's chest. Was Diego living life on his own terms, or was he so bound by expectations that he was sacrificing his own happiness to keep someone else's dream alive?

"I can't let it fail." Diego's voice was barely audible over the sounds of the brushes and the horses' breathing. "The Cruz family is this ranch—the two are entwined."

"I know it seems that way," Wyatt said carefully. "But deep down, I hope you realize that's not true. You don't have to carry on if it's not what you want."

"I do, though," he replied. "This is my legacy. I want to preserve it and pass it on to my children someday. But we have to change with the world. I don't want to be the one to sink us because we remained stuck in the old ways."

"I think your sister feels the same way." He'd seen it on her face when they'd talked about why she'd come back. Isabel loved this land, loved her family. She was proud of the history of the ranch, and he knew she was determined to do her part to keep it going.

Even though he thought drilling was the wrong choice.

Diego nodded. "She does. We just disagree on how to move forward."

Wyatt realized he had to be careful here. He wanted

to help bridge the distance between two people he loved, but he didn't want to insert himself into the middle of their relationship. So he opted to remain neutral.

"I know you will both figure out a compromise."

Ajax let out a deep sigh as Wyatt began running the soft brush over his body. This was the horse's favorite part—he loved to have the spot just behind his ears brushed. "In the meantime," Wyatt said, "we need to figure out how to stop these attacks."

"I know," Diego agreed. "I've already called the sheriff's office. They're coming out first thing in the morning to talk to us."

"How did they react when you told them we've removed the traps and disposed of the carcasses?"

"Not well," Diego admitted. "But I pushed back and told them I couldn't leave the site as-is. It's too dangerous for the rest of the herd, or any unwitting hiker who trespasses on our property. The deputy calmed down when I told him I'd taken photos of everything, and that we'd give them the traps." He began to wipe Miel's face with a soft rag. "The truth is," he said, lowering his voice even further, "I'm not convinced the sheriff or his people are going to be able to do much."

"Why's that?"

His friend shrugged. "Think about it. Those devices have been outside, exposed to the elements. I doubt they'll get any kind of fingerprints from them, and even if they do, if the person doing this isn't in their database, it's not going to matter."

"That's true," Wyatt allowed.

"And besides," Diego continued. "I think they know it's going to be next to impossible to find out who the culprit is. The area is so remote, and with no clear suspects or motive, it's hard to know where to start."

"Have you been watching those cop shows again?" Wyatt teased.

"Yeah," he admitted. "But you know I'm right." Diego grabbed a hoof pick and began to inspect Miel's feet. "I did tell them to check out Gabriel, though."

"You think he's involved?" Wyatt considered the possibility, but things just didn't add up.

"I do. I can't put my finger on it, but I think he's part of this."

"That doesn't make sense." Wyatt bent at the waist and lifted one of Ajax's feet, checking his hooves for embedded rocks or damage. "He's trying to claim a part of the business—he said himself he wants you to buy him out. Why would he try to sabotage the ranch, when that only hurts his bottom line?"

Diego shook his head. "I don't know. But I know he's connected."

"You just don't like him."

Diego conceded the point with a nod. "Never claimed otherwise. But can you blame me?"

"Not really." Gabriel might indeed be part of the

Cruz family, but he could have done a better job of introducing himself. "If you ever want to talk about it, I'm here. You know that, right?"

"Yeah," Diego said. "I appreciate it."

They finished grooming the horses in silence, then put them in their respective stalls and topped off the food and water.

Knowing their time alone was drawing to a close, Wyatt decided to broach a more delicate subject. "So... Now that you know about me and Isabel, are we still cool?"

Diego flashed a grin as they wiped down their tack. "Yeah. I'm still adjusting to the idea of you and my sister, but it's all good."

Relief washed over Wyatt as he realized he wasn't going to have to choose between his lover and his best friend. "I'm glad to hear it."

After hanging everything up, they headed for the barn entrance.

Ruben was there, hanging up his saddle blanket to air out overnight. Diego clapped him on the shoulder. "Thanks for your help today."

"Yup."

"Come on to the house. Join us for dinner."

Ruben glanced in the direction of the big house. Light blazed from its windows, giving the place a gilded look in the twilight. "Probably shouldn't," he said. "It wouldn't be nice to surprise Maria with another mouth to feed."

Diego laughed. "I can promise you, she has made enough food to supply an army."

"I'm filthy—"

"We all are. No more excuses. Join us, please. You've more than earned a hot meal for your efforts today."

Ruben hesitated then nodded.

The three of them walked to the house and then went their separate ways to wash up before dinner.

Wyatt poked his head into Isabel's room and found her sitting on the bed, her laptop open in front of her. She was frowning as she stared at the screen.

"Hey."

She glanced up, relief washing over her face when she saw him. "You're back!" She jumped up, crossed the room in a few strides. Without hesitation, she threw herself against his chest and wrapped her arms around his body.

"I'm here," he said, dropping his head to stick his nose in her hair. He inhaled deeply, the scent of her shampoo replacing the odor of death that still lingered in his sinuses. "What are you working on?"

"Hmm?" She glanced back at the computer. "Just trying to organize my thoughts. I'll tell you about it later." Her hands cupped the back of his neck and she drew him down for a kiss. Her mouth was hot and hungry against his, and she kissed him with a desperation that told him how worried she'd been all day.

"I'm fine," he said once they'd come up for air. He

touched her cheek lightly, aware of just how dirty he still was. "Everything is all right."

"I want you to go back to the park tomorrow," she said. Her brown eyes were serious as she stared up at him. "I don't want you involved in this any longer."

Wyatt shook his head. "Come on," he said.

"What? Where are we going?" She followed him into the hall.

"To the bathroom. I'm a mess, and I'm not going to have this argument with you while I still reek of today's work."

"Oh." She followed him inside the small room, shut the door behind them and leaned against the sink. "I don't see why this has to be an argument," she said. "You need to go back to work—you said so yourself this morning."

Wyatt turned on the shower and stripped off his clothes, gratified to hear Isabel's breath hitch as he stepped free of his pants and boxers. "My job is not something you need to worry about." He stuck his hand under the spray, found it hot. Pulling the curtain back, he stepped inside. "Care to join me?"

She swallowed hard. "No. No—that's okay."

He shrugged. "Lady's choice." He jerked the curtain shut and stepped fully under the spray. The hot water felt like heaven to his tired muscles and his skin rejoiced as the dirt and sweat and grime began to rinse away.

"As I was saying." She'd raised her voice to be heard over the shower. Wyatt grinned and reached for the shampoo. Isabel was nothing if not determined.

"I want you to go back to work tomorrow."

"Tired of me already?" he teased, lathering up.

"No." He closed his eyes, picturing her expression. He'd bet a month's paycheck she was standing there wearing that look of prim annoyance combined with fond exasperation.

"Then why are you so desperate for me to leave?" He stuck his head under the water to rinse off the shampoo.

"I don't want you to put yourself in danger for us."

Ah, there was the root of the problem. She was scared.

He peered around the curtain. She was staring at the floor, gnawing on her lower lip. "Shouldn't that be my decision?"

She jumped at the sound of his voice so close to her. "No."

"No?" he repeated, raising one eyebrow.

Isabel shook her head. "I know you, Wyatt. You'll do anything to help us, even at your own expense. I can't have you get hurt. I'd never forgive myself."

He reached for her, water dripping from his arm to land on the mat with soft plopping sounds. She took his hand and let him pull her closer. "I'm not going to get hurt," he promised.

"I want to believe that," she said. "But…things are getting worse."

"I know." He'd thought of little else all day. "Do

you honestly think I'd walk away while this is going on? There is no chance I'm going to leave you when things here are so precarious."

"I don't want to lose you." Her voice was hardly more than a whisper. "We've only just found each other again."

He smiled, warmth spreading through his chest as she echoed his thoughts. "You won't. Come here." He tugged gently on her hand.

Isabel's eyes went wide. "What, you mean in there?" She'd declined his first invitation, but he could tell she was considering this one.

Wyatt nodded. She looked uncertain, but she took off her clothes and stepped over the ledge of the tub to join him.

He drew the curtain closed behind her, further sealing them off from the rest of the house. Then he pulled her close, loving the feel of her skin against his own.

"You're not going to lose me." He captured her mouth, kissing her deeply as he ran his hands down her body. "I'm not going anywhere."

"You'd better not." Isabel gripped his shoulders, her short fingernails digging into his skin. Her earlier worry seemed to be fading, replaced by a growing passion.

Her hands slid across his shoulders, over his chest and down his stomach until she wrapped her fingers around him in a clear gesture of possession. His hips thrust involuntarily, seeking more friction from her touch. She made a low humming sound and began to stroke him, gently at first, then with an increasing pressure that made his eyes roll back in his head.

He could have stayed like that forever, but the need to claim her drove him forward. Wyatt shifted their bodies, shuffling back until he pressed Isabel against the tile. She let out a soft cry as her skin made contact with the cold surface, but he was too far gone to care.

Before she had a chance to react, he dropped to his knees and lifted one of her legs, hooking it over his shoulder.

"Wyatt!" His name came out on a gasp as he leaned forward, using his lips and tongue to explore her most private places.

He felt her muscles tense, heard her cries of pleasure. Her hands landed on his head and she gripped his hair tightly, anchoring him in place.

Not that he intended to move anytime soon.

He couldn't stand for her to be afraid, so he used his body to chase her fears away. He wanted—no, needed—to fill her with pleasure, to leave her limp and satisfied, with no room for doubt or worry.

Something primal rose in his chest as he tasted her. She squirmed against his mouth, her breath coming in hard pants above him. "Mine," he growled against her core.

"Yes," she gasped. "Always."

He pulled her to the floor of the tub, the water

raining down on them from above. She was on her knees facing him, mouth slack with pleasure. She reached for him, but he wasn't done with her yet.

"Turn around."

She blinked then a sensuous smile spread across her face as she did what he instructed.

Wyatt entered her slowly, fighting against the urge to take her hard and fast. There would be time for that later; right now he was totally focused on her.

He leaned over her, sheltering her from the shower spray as he settled into an easy rhythm. "You belong to me," he said in her ear. "And I belong to you. Nothing will change that."

"Promise?" Her voice was tight and he could tell she was on the edge of release.

"I promise." He reached around to the front of her body and stroked her sensitive nub with the pad of his thumb. She jerked under him and let out a soft cry.

"I'll never let you go," he said, feeling her muscles grow tense with pleasure as he continued to move.

Her core gripped him tightly, inner muscles spasming as she reached her climax. "I love you." The declaration tumbled out of her as she came, her back arching against him.

The words shot straight to his heart, burrowing deep into his soul. He felt his own release approach and, mindful that he wasn't wearing a condom, slipped free from her body. Even though they were no longer joined, he still kept his arms around her to maintain the contact between them. "I love you, too," he said, his mouth next to her ear. "Always have. Always will."

Chapter 12

They were the last ones to make it to the dinner table, but no one said anything about their late arrival.

Isabel took her seat next to Wyatt, her body still thrumming with the aftershocks of pleasure. She'd never been so thoroughly *possessed* before; all her previous sexual experiences had been nice, but nowhere near as intense as what they'd just shared in the shower. Wyatt had claimed her, body and soul, and offered up his heart in exchange.

It was the best bargain she'd ever made.

The bathroom had never been her idea of a romantic location, but she hadn't wanted to leave. They'd created a cocoon for themselves, blocking out the rest of the world with its attendant worries and stresses. The intensity of those stolen moments took her breath away and helped to ease the sting of knowing they could have spent the last ten years in each other's arms.

Would she ever get used to being with Wyatt? Would there come a point when she no longer felt sparks of sensation every time he touched her? Or was the magic between them strong enough to last a lifetime?

There was only one way to find out.

She slid a glance in his direction, watching from the corner of her eye as he spooned beans onto his plate. He moved with a graceful economy, his hands gentle as they held Maria's aging china. Heat bloomed in her chest as she considered the contrast between Wyatt's banked power and his careful gestures, recalling other, more intimate times when his strength had been deliciously overwhelming.

"Did you have any trouble today?" Abuelo asked Diego.

His question snapped Isabel out of her reverie, snuffing her arousal and forcing her thoughts back to the present. As much as she wished she could revel in her newfound reconnection with Wyatt, there were real problems she needed to consider.

Diego shook his head. "We got it done." He nodded at Wyatt and Ruben. "Everyone worked hard." Then he turned to Isabel. "Your horse is getting better. She didn't shy away from the blood as much this time."

"I'm glad to hear it," she said. "I knew she had it in her."

Abuelo nodded. "I stayed busy myself today. I had Isabel take me to Alpine."

Diego narrowed his eyes slightly. "Why's that?"

"For the DNA test."

Diego leaned back in his chair with a sigh. "I would have done that," he said, his tone slightly scolding. "There was no need for you to make the trip."

Abuelo shrugged. "It had to be done. We need to know for certain."

"When will you have the results?" asked Wyatt.

"Tomorrow. They're expediting them."

A clatter at the end of the table made everyone turn. Ruben picked up his fork with an apologetic grimace. "Sorry. My hands are stiff."

Maria waved off his apology and handed him the plate of tortillas with a smile.

Diego nodded to himself. "Well…" He scooped up another bite. "We need to decide what to do next."

"We also need to give the energy company an answer," Isabel said. She hated to talk business at the table, but this was the first time they'd all been together today without dead cattle and cyanide traps vying for attention. "They've presented us with another offer," she continued. "It's higher than before."

She'd been pleasantly surprised when she'd opened the folder the company representatives had left earlier in the day. It seemed her earlier fears that they were going to rescind their offer had been incorrect.

Diego huffed. "I guess they're not giving up."

"How much higher?" Abuelo asked.

She named the figure in the paperwork the men had handed over this morning. Everyone gasped.

"Damn," Diego muttered. "That's some serious shi—"

"Mijo," Maria cut him off.

"Sorry." He ran a hand through his hair then reached for his beer. "I suppose you're even more eager to accept now?"

Isabel nodded. "I think we have to. I don't know if they'll increase their offer again. They might even take it off the table entirely, if we continue to stall."

"They won't," Diego proclaimed. "I've been talking to a lawyer who specializes in these kinds of cases. She thinks the only way they can drill on our land is if we let them. They can't have the state pressure us, or use eminent domain to seize our property."

"When did you do this?" Abuelo sounded surprised.

"Shortly after they made the first offer," Diego replied. "I remember what happened with the pipeline a few years ago, how the state swooped in and took over tracts of land from the owners. She told me in these cases, drilling on private property is considered a separate category from pipeline construction and operation. Since we own the land outright, the company can't force us to do anything."

Isabel saw her brother's resolve strengthen, and her own frustration grew. "I'm glad our property is safe from seizure, but that doesn't solve our revenue problem. I still think we should sell the rights. Maybe we could put in a condition, like they can't set up a well for a certain number of months?"

"No." Diego shook his head. "Don't you see? If we give them an inch, they will wind up taking a mile. We cannot be short-sighted about this."

"Then what do you suggest?" Isabel dropped her fork; it landed with a clang against the plate. "We can't keep going on the way we are. Something has got to change."

She glanced to Wyatt in mute appeal, but his frown told her he wasn't on her side.

This is just the beginning, she realized with a small shock. She didn't mind being on the opposite side of an issue as Wyatt. But what if this was only the first in a long line of incompatibilities? What if they couldn't agree on any of life's major decisions? How could they build a relationship when they couldn't even find the middle ground here?

They'd had a one-night stand ten years ago, followed by a quick jump back into a physical relationship, their emotions heightened by the jeopardy she'd faced and the crisis her family was in. That had muddied her otherwise clear thinking. She needed to slow down, to consider things more carefully. Just because they'd happily reconnected and righted the wrong that had kept them apart didn't mean they were destined for each other, or truly compatible.

They were physically in sync, there was no doubt about that. But Isabel needed more than just great sex. And while she didn't want a partner who agreed with her every word, she also didn't want to spend most of her time arguing with him, either.

A sense of disappointment sliced through her as she looked at the faces around the table. Diego had never thought the well was a good idea, but Abuelo had at least pretended to consider it. Now, though, she could tell her grandfather was more in agreement with her brother.

That was fine—she understood she wasn't going to win every argument. But what hurt the most was the fact that not only was her family ignoring the economic realities the ranch was facing, they expected her to come up with a compromise all on her own. Neither her brother nor her grandfather—nor Wyatt, for that matter—had suggested an alternative that would help the ranch stay afloat. And Wyatt had promised to help come up with ideas.

After a few minutes of silence, it became clear no one had anything to say.

"Fine." She spoke quietly, determined to keep her emotions under control. "I understand you don't want to sell the mineral rights. But unless one of us comes up with another plan, and fast, we're not going to have a choice."

Unable to sit there any longer, she pushed back

from the table and gathered her empty plate and silverware. Then she walked away without saying another word.

Wyatt knocked softly on Isabel's bedroom door, uncertain of his welcome. She'd tried to hide her emotions at the dinner table, but it was clear to anyone with eyes that she was upset over her brother's refusal to budge in light of the new offering.

And he knew his own lack of support had disappointed her, as well.

"Come in."

He pushed the door open and found her once again sitting on the bed with her laptop open. When she didn't look up, he stepped inside and closed the door behind him.

"What are you working on?"

She shook her head. "I don't even know. I'm trying to come up with some plan to save the ranch, because apparently I'm the only one who is capable of thinking about this."

"You know that's not true." He walked to the bed and sat next to her, wanting to comfort her. But would she welcome his touch?

There was only one way to find out. He placed his hand on her shoulder, stroked lightly down her back.

She didn't shrug away from him, but she didn't lean into him, either.

It was a start.

"I know you're frustrated," he said. "But this is a

complicated situation. You can't expect to just figure it out in a matter of minutes."

"I've been working on it for weeks," she muttered.

"Yeah, but you've been stressed," he countered. "Hard to think straight when you're upset."

"What happened to your earlier offer?" She turned to face him, challenge glinting in her eyes. "You said you'd try to help me come up with an alternative plan."

"I meant it," he said.

She arched one eyebrow. "Feel free to jump in anytime."

Wyatt ignored her sarcasm, knowing it was born of frustration. "Well, how about you give me some information first? What kind of numbers are we talking about here?"

She gave him a rundown of the financial status of the ranch. The magnitude of the problem became clear as she spoke, settling over his shoulders like a heavy blanket. And he wasn't even part of the family. How much worse must the pressure feel for her and Diego? They had enough money to keep going in the short term—a very *short* short term—but if something wasn't done soon, they would be sinking deeper and deeper into the red with every passing month.

"Wow," he said when she was done.

She nodded. "So that's what we're dealing with. You can see now why I'm so eager to accept the fracking offer."

"I do," he said. "But… I still don't think that's the answer."

"Of course not," she muttered, turning away.

He reached for her, unwilling to let her shut him out. "Hey." He placed his fingers under her chin and turned her head until she faced him again. "What's this really about?"

She shook her head but he wasn't going to let her off the hook so easily.

"Talk to me, Isabel."

"Maybe this isn't such a good idea," she said finally.

Her words sent a chill skittering down his spine. He got the feeling she wasn't talking about the ranch plans anymore. "What do you mean?"

"You and me." She gestured between them. "Us. Maybe we're better off as friends. Or at least starting as friends. This has been so fast."

Wyatt's heart began to crack but he refused to let it show. "What makes you say that?"

She shoved off the bed, began to pace the room. "Maybe we're just not compatible," she said, gesturing with her hands as she spoke. "This is a perfect example—I think we need to sell the mineral rights, you don't. We're both working from the same data set, yet we've drawn completely opposite conclusions. Maybe that tells us something about how we'd be together as a couple."

"And you think that's a deal-breaker?" He fought

to keep his tone neutral. Was she really suggesting they break up over this damn offer?

She shook her head. "What I think is that it's a sign of things to come. If we can't see eye-to-eye on something as straightforward as this, what makes you think we'll be on the same page when it comes to more complicated stuff, like kids or jobs?"

"Wait a minute." Wyatt held up a hand, needing her to take a breath. Needing one himself, for that matter. "That's an awfully big leap. I don't mean to prove your point, but I have to say I disagree."

She smiled, but there was no joy in it. "I'm not happy about this, either. But I don't think we can move forward until we learn more about each other, take things more slowly. More…naturally. I don't want to spend my life in a constant argument with the person who's supposed to be my partner."

"Neither do I." He spread his hands wide. "See? We're on the same page there." It was another lame attempt at humor, but he needed to snap her out of this mood, to help her see how unreasonable she was being. Of course they were going to disagree on things—how boring would their life together be if they saw the world in exactly the same way?

That didn't mean they were doomed to a relationship of constant conflict, though. Why couldn't she recognize that? Sure, things had progressed fast with them, but not really when you thought of the ten years they should have had together if not for misunderstandings.

Isabel shook her head. "I wish I shared your optimism. I just… I need more time."

Wyatt's stomach dropped. "All right," he said quietly. He wasn't going to beg her to be with him. But before he walked away and gave her the space she wanted, there was one thing he needed to know.

"Earlier in the shower. You said you loved me. Did you mean it or was it just the sex talking?"

She looked away, her cheeks turning pink under his gaze. "I wouldn't lie about something like that," she said finally.

"Good." Her answer should have made him feel better, but instead it only fed his frustration. Why was she pumping the brakes on their relationship now, when only hours before they'd been totally connected, body and soul? "I meant what I said, too. I do love you, Isabel Cruz. And I'll give you some time to figure out what you want. But I won't wait forever."

With that, he stood and walked to the door, needing to get out of there before she could see his heart breaking.

Chapter 13

"Isabel."

She came awake with a start, jerking at the strange touch.

"It's okay," said Diego softly. "It's just me."

She glanced instinctively to the other side of the bed, but Wyatt wasn't there. That's right—he was sleeping in the guest room. Her heart sank at the reminder of their argument and its aftermath, but she pushed aside her disappointment and focused on the here and now.

"Delivery problems?"

Her brother nodded. "Give me two minutes," she whispered.

Diego left the room on silent feet as she slid out of bed. Moving in the dark, she exchanged her nightshirt for a pair of old scrubs, then gathered her boots and stepped into the hall.

The clock downstairs chimed three times as she shoved her feet into her boots. "Perfect timing," she muttered. "As usual."

Thank you, evolution, she thought wryly as she descended the stairs, trying to be quiet about it. Veterinary obstetrical complications went hand in hand with the darkness, thanks to horses and cows having a tendency to wait for the cover of night to go into labor. It was a trait that had served them well when they were still free-ranging animals who needed to avoid drawing the attention of nearby predators. But now that they enjoyed the benefits of domestication, it was hell on their human caretakers.

She grabbed her heavy coat from the hook by the door and jogged down the porch steps. The night air held a chill, but she knew from experience the calving barn itself would be cold.

"What have we got?" she said as she arrived.

Diego turned at the sound of her voice. "Three first timers," he said, indicating the scene with a nod. "Two showing signs of distress."

She walked over to her brother, who was standing next to an animal that was clearly agitated. A quick glance at her tail end revealed the problem. "Nose first, huh?"

"Yeah."

"Get her in the chute." She removed a pair of arm-length plastic gloves from her bag and glanced at a second cow. "What's her story?"

"I think the calf is coming out backward," replied Peter, one of the younger ranch hands.

Isabel trotted over to check out the situation herself. Calves were usually born front feet first, followed by the head and the rest of the body. But as she got closer, she recognized this one was indeed flipped around.

"Okay," she said, noting that both Peter and the cow seemed anxious about the situation. "See how the feet are poking out?"

The young man nodded, swallowing hard.

"That's actually a good sign," she said. "I'm just going to do a quick check…" She inserted her arm as she spoke, palpating the calf's anatomy to make sure it was positioned in such a way that it could come out.

"All right," she said, finishing up. "This isn't ideal, but I don't think the calf is in any distress right now. What I need you to do is to keep an eye on things while I go help out over there. You should start to see more of the legs emerge soon, but if they come out fast and you see the belly I need to know right away."

"Do I need to pull or anything?"

"No!"

Peter jumped at her exclamation.

"No," she repeated, softening her voice. "Don't pull on the legs at all. I'll be back in a few minutes."

She stripped off the used glove and replaced it with a fresh one as she approached the first cow. "All right, mama," she said, stepping behind the animal. "Let's get this done."

She set to work, pushing, twisting, coaxing and pleading. It was a tough job but, after several minutes, she'd managed to push the calf back into the uterus and move it into a better position for birth. "Try again," she said, patting the cow on the rump.

Relief flared in Peter's eyes as she started in his direction again. "How are we doing here?"

"Okay? I think?" His voice shook a little, which made Isabel smile as she replaced her glove once more.

"First time?"

He nodded, wiped the sweat from his forehead with his sleeve. "Is it that obvious?"

"It's going to be fine. I was terrified during my first calving season, as well. You'll get used to it."

She walked over to the laboring cow, assessing the situation as she drew closer. The calf was making progress, but not as much as she'd hoped to see.

"Okay, Peter, I'm going to need you to help me."

"Yeah?" He rubbed his hands on his jeans. "What can I do?"

"Remember how I told you earlier not to pull?" He nodded. "Well, believe it or not, now I need you to help me pull."

"Seriously?" He chuckled nervously.

"Yep," she confirmed. "If this calf stays in there much longer, it will suffocate. Let's help her out."

She grabbed one leg, showed Peter where to grip the other. "All right. On my count, I need a strong and steady tug. One, two, three!"

Working together, they helped draw the calf out of its mother's body. She landed on the floor of the barn with a dull thud and, as Isabel had suspected, didn't move right away.

"Keep going," she said, urging Peter to help her pull the calf a few feet away. They arranged her in a sitting position to help her breathe. Isabel could feel a pulse, but if this baby didn't start breathing well soon, it wasn't going to last. She knelt by the animal's head and grabbed a stalk of straw, which she then unceremoniously shoved up the calf's nose.

"What are you doing?" Peter crouched next to her, his eyes as wide as dinner plates.

"Trying to get her to cough." She used her free hand to wipe the calf's nose and mouth clear of mucus and fluids. "Come on," she muttered.

The calf bobbed her head, trying to get away from the straw. After a few seconds, she let out a soft bleat of protest at her rough treatment.

"Good job, little one." Isabel gave her a scratch behind the ears then glanced at Peter. "Keep an eye on her for me. After a few minutes, you can put mom and baby in one of the stalls."

"What about the rest?" He gestured to the cow, who was craning her neck in an attempt to see around the edges of the metal chute that held her still. "Isn't there more that has to come out?"

"She'll deliver the placenta later," Isabel said, getting to her feet. "It doesn't come out right away." She started to cross the barn to return to the first cow then paused. "Peter?"

He glanced up from his spot by the calf. "Yes?"

"Great job."

His smile was dazzling. "Thanks."

She made it back to Diego. "How are we doing?"

"So far so good," he said. "Front hooves are peeking out a little with each contraction."

"Excellent." She took advantage of the temporary lull to check on the third cow, who was doing nicely. Isabel stayed just outside the pen, watching as the animal delivered her first calf. It plopped to the ground and immediately began to squirm. The mother turned and started to lick her baby clean in a textbook example of a calving.

"Nice job," she said softly, not wanting to disturb the pair.

"Two out, one to go," she said as she returned to Diego's side.

He nodded. "'Tis the season," he replied.

They watched the cow for a few moments as her labor progressed. Sure enough, a pair of hooves emerged, followed quickly by thin legs.

Isabel felt some of the tension leave her muscles. "Looking good."

She continued to watch the cow, wrinkling her

nose as an acrid odor began to overpower the mingled aromas of blood, dung and birth scents hanging in the air.

She frowned, sniffed again. "Diego? Do you smell that?"

He took a deep breath. "Smells like—"

"Smoke!" Peter yelled. Isabel turned to find him pointing at the far corner of the barn, his expression panicked.

Wisps of gray smoke hugged the wall as they rose into the air.

"Oh my God," Isabel said. Her heart leaped into her throat and for an endless second she couldn't move.

Diego cursed. "Grab a fire extinguisher." He darted for the entrance, where a pair of fire extinguishers hung from hooks on the wall.

But as Isabel discovered when she skidded to a stop behind her brother, they weren't there.

"Where are they?" she yelled. The smoke was growing thicker now, the color darker and more ominous.

"I don't know." Diego jogged to the doors and pushed, trying to open them to the fresh night air.

But they didn't budge.

"What do we do?" Peter joined them, looking like he wanted to cry.

He's so young, Isabel realized in a sudden moment of clarity. When had Diego started hiring children?

"Help me push," Diego instructed. Peter threw

himself against the wide doors and Isabel pushed on the other side of Diego. But their combined efforts still weren't enough to dislodge the doors.

The air was growing heavy with soot and smoke. The cows were getting scared—their moos sounded increasingly frantic.

"We have to get them out of here," Isabel said.

"Forget the cows," Peter said. "What about us?" He glanced at the walls, which sported a row of small windows about six feet off the ground.

Diego grabbed her hand and half led, half dragged her over to the wall. "Can you fit through that?" He picked up a nearby broom and used it to smash the glass. The growing smoke began to stream out of the now open window, obscuring the night sky.

Isabel shook her head. "I'm not leaving you."

"You don't have a choice," her brother shot back.

"I'll go," Peter injected frantically.

Isabel nodded. "Good. We'll boost you up. Crawl through, then go to the entrance and get those doors open. Diego and I will free the cattle."

Diego glared at her. "It should be you, sis."

"We're wasting time here." She leaned forward, cupping her hands to provide a spot for Peter's foot. After a second, Diego followed suit.

Peter planted his boot in her hands and pushed, launching himself up. She and Diego straightened together, helping to lift Peter so he could reach the window.

The young man shoved his arms and head through

the gap. He hung there for an endless second before wiggling the rest of the way through. Once his boots disappeared from view, Isabel turned and grabbed Diego's shirt.

"Release the cow from the chute. I'm going after the two new moms."

She didn't give her brother a chance to respond before stepping into the thick cloud of smoke hanging in the air. Her eyes burned as she squinted to make out her surroundings. The cries of the panicked cows echoed in the barn, making it hard to pinpoint exactly where they were.

Working from memory, she picked a direction and set off, keeping her eyes on the floor in the hope of finding a landmark. She shrugged out of her jacket and tied it around her nose and mouth. It didn't stop the smoke from coating her mouth with an acrid film, but it was better than nothing.

Whether through sheer luck or divine intervention, she stumbled into the pen holding the cow and her breeched calf. The baby was on her feet now, standing close to her mother's legs for shelter and comfort.

Isabel knelt and grabbed the calf, pulling it close to her chest. She stood and then snagged the cow's lead line with her hand. A quick glance around revealed an orange glow to her left—

Flames, she realized with a flash of terror.

She put the fire behind her and set off, hoping she was headed in the right direction.

Every step was a battle. Her throat grew tighter with every heartbeat and her lungs felt raw and ragged, as though she was inhaling ground glass. But she pushed forward, unwilling to let these innocent creatures die a horrible death.

"Isabel!"

Diego's voice rang out in the din. "Where are you?"

"Coming." She said it as loudly as she could manage, but her brother obviously hadn't heard her as he continued to shout her name. After what seemed like an eternity, she saw his boots.

"I'm here," she said.

She couldn't see his face, but suddenly the calf was taken from her. Then Diego pulled her forward, pressing her face to a crack in the door. "Breathe," he commanded.

A trickle of cool air drifted across her forehead in a tantalizing caress. She pulled the fabric away from her nose and inhaled, but it wasn't enough to clear her lungs.

Diego kept his hand on the back of her head, forcing her to breathe what little fresh air she could get. After a moment, she broke free and turned back. "Why aren't the doors open yet?"

"I don't know." He had to yell now, as the crackles and pops of spreading flames added to the cacophony of sound. "Something's got to be wrong."

Suddenly there was a loud smack against the other side of the doors. The muffled sound of voices rose above the din, but she couldn't make out individual words.

"Someone's there," she said, relief stealing over her.

But a quick glance behind them showed a wall of advancing orange. Tongues of flame licked up the walls of the barn, bringing a heat that was quickly becoming unbearable. Isabel jerked as something blindingly hot landed on her head. She rubbed frantically at the spot, dislodging a smoldering ember that had drifted down from the ceiling.

Diego pounded on the door then doubled over as a coughing spasm took hold. Isabel tugged his face over to the crack of air, trying to keep her own breaths shallow. A clawing sense of panic added to the claustrophobic smoke and heat eddying around them. She closed her eyes, summoned up the image of Wyatt's face in an effort to stay calm. Why, oh why, had she gone to sleep still angry with him?

Her heart beat hard against her ribs, as though trying to leave her behind in a bid to escape the fire. All at once, she realized she'd been worried about all the wrong things. She'd been so focused on saving the ranch, she'd put her relationships at risk. But what was the ranch worth if she didn't have her family and Wyatt?

"Hold on!"

She heard those words clearly through the door, though they offered little reassurance. Help had definitely arrived. But was it too late?

* * *

It was the clanging of the dinner bell that woke him.

Wyatt sat up in the darkness, rubbing his eyes. He reached for Isabel, only to discover she wasn't there. Oh, right. After their argument, he'd gone to sleep in the guest bedroom.

His chest ached as he recalled the look on her face as she'd told him she needed more time. She'd seemed simultaneously lost and hurt, and he'd wanted nothing more than to hold her.

But his own heart had been breaking, so he'd respected her wishes and left. If it hadn't been full dark at the time, he would have saddled Ajax and headed back to Big Bend. But he knew better than to risk his safety to assuage his pride. So he'd climbed into the guest room bed, determined to leave at the first sign of dawn.

He glanced out the window—still dark. Then he heard the voices outside—a chorus of shouts and cries of alarm. One word pierced the residual fog of sleep clouding his mind.

"Fire!"

His body reacted before his mind fully realized what was happening. He scrambled out of bed and yanked on pants, boots and a shirt before racing from the room.

"Isabel?" He knocked on her door, needing to know she was sleeping safely in her room. But when she didn't answer after a few seconds, he twisted the knob and pushed inside.

Her bed was empty. Was she attending a delivery? Or was something more dangerous going on?

He hit the front porch in record time and the sight that greeted him turned his guts to water.

The calving barn was ablaze, the back half of the building lit up like a Roman candle. The flames were racing to the front of the building, where a group of men were gathered, shouting and jostling each other as they worked on something. A few others were clustered around a heap lying on the ground a few feet away.

A body?

He wasn't aware of moving, didn't register the cold against his skin as he sprinted for the barn. His instincts told him Isabel needed him and he wasn't going to let her down.

The soles of his boots slid on the dirt as he skidded to a stop by the object on the ground. He dropped to his knees next to the small form, his heart in his throat as he reached out with shaking hands.

It wasn't Isabel—he realized it as soon as he touched the person's arm. The young man moaned and rolled onto his back, reaching up to clutch his head.

"What happened?" Wyatt said. He had to yell to be heard over the roar of flames.

"They pushed me out the window," the young man said, wincing as he spoke. "I came around to open the doors, but someone hit me."

"Who pushed you out the window?" Wyatt said. *Please, no...*

"Diego and Doc Isabel," the kid said. "They're still inside."

For a second, Wyatt couldn't hear anything over the rush of blood in his ears. Then a deafening boom split the air. He turned in time to see the back half of the barn collapse, shooting a blizzard of sparks into the night sky.

He tried to scream Isabel's name, but the lump in his throat blocked the sound. Driven by desperation, he half stumbled, half crawled over to the barn doors. A cluster of ranch hands was there, yanking and pulling and yelling as they tried to gain access to the barn.

Wyatt stared in disbelief at the chain wrapped through the handles, sealing the doors so no one could get in or out of the barn.

My God, he thought. *This is no accident.*

"Move!" commanded a loud voice.

He turned to see Ruben approaching with a pair of bolt cutters. The firelight glinted off his belt buckle as he leaned forward and started cutting the links of the chain.

Wyatt fought the urge to grab the cutters, knowing the other man was moving as quickly as he could under the circumstances. But Isabel was inside, dammit, and he had to get to her!

After what seemed like an eternity, the chain clattered to the ground. The group yanked the doors open and thick black smoke belched into the sky.

A cow shot through the door, a calf hanging half out of her body. Someone grabbed her lead line and led her off to the side, away from the chaos. It was the most surreal thing Wyatt had ever seen, but he didn't have time to think about it now. The heifer was followed quickly by two more, but he saw no human figures stumbling out of the inferno.

Wyatt fought his way to the front of the scrum, determined to find Isabel. The smoke made his eyes sting and his lungs tightened in protest, but he pressed on, needing to get to her.

"Diego!" He heard the shouts of the other ranch hands, felt a spurt of relief at the fact they'd found his friend. But where was Isabel?

He tripped over something a few feet into the barn. Unable to see, he reached down to feel the obstacle.

It was an arm. Isabel's arm.

His heart pounded hard as he knelt to gather her up. There were two newborn calves next to her, their still damp hides now covered in ashes and soot.

She stirred as he stood. "The babies," she gasped out, reaching for the closest one.

"We'll get them," he promised. "Don't worry." He turned and headed for the exit, yelling for help as he moved.

Three ranch hands were there in a matter of seconds. One of them reached for Isabel, but Wyatt gripped her closer. He wasn't about to let her go.

"Get the calves," he yelled, jerking his head back. There was no way of knowing if they were going to survive, but he wanted to be able to tell Isabel they'd at least tried to save them.

Wyatt didn't stop moving until they were well away from the barn. He carefully laid Isabel on the ground, trying not to jostle her too much.

She was covered in soot and her clothes sported numerous small holes where sparks had burned through. He yanked the jacket away from her neck— she must have tried to tie it around her nose and mouth to block out the smoke. If the stains on her skin were any indication, it hadn't helped.

"Come on, Izzy," he said, using the nickname he knew she'd hated. "Wake up and breathe for me."

Wyatt didn't want to think about how much damage the smoke had done to her lungs, especially following so close on the heels of her cyanide exposure. The movements of her chest were far too shallow for his liking, but without an oxygen tank, there was nothing he could do for her at this point.

His fingers found the pulse at her wrist and registered the feel of the steady beat there. It eased his mind somewhat to know her heart was still going strong, but he wouldn't fully relax until she'd been treated at a hospital.

Her eyes fluttered open. Even in the hazy glow of the fire, Wyatt could see they were completely bloodshot. She squinted up at him. "Wyatt?" Her voice was little more than a rasp and his throat ached in sympathy.

"I'm here." He gripped her hand and leaned over her, placing his face directly above hers so she could see him without effort. "You're okay. You're out."

She swallowed. "Diego?"

"He's out, too. You're both going to be okay." In truth, he had no idea how her brother was doing. But he didn't want to her to worry. Not now.

Isabel tried to nod. She moved her lips again but Wyatt couldn't make out what she was trying to say.

"Shh," he told her. "Just rest."

She frowned, undeterred.

Knowing she wouldn't stop until she'd gotten her message across, Wyatt leaned down until his ear was hovering just above her lips.

"The cows."

He fought the absurd urge to laugh. They were in the middle of an emergency, she was seriously injured, and yet she was still worried about the damn cows?

"I saw three heifers run out of the barn," he replied. "One was in the middle of giving birth. We pulled two calves out with you."

She relaxed, a smile forming at the corners of her mouth. "That's good."

Indeed it was, because there was no way in hell Wyatt was stepping back into that furnace in search of a wayward animal. He loved nature as much as the next person, but he had his limits.

Isabel was speaking again.

"Save your voice," he suggested. "Whatever it is, you can tell me later."

She shook her head, frowning up at him.

"All right," he said, smoothing the hair back from her face. "What is it?"

"I'm sorry," she rasped. "I was wrong."

Her words sliced through him, bringing tears to his eyes. As if he gave a damn about their earlier fight?

"Shh," he said. "You don't need to apologize to me."

"I do," she choked out. "I love you."

Wyatt wanted to kiss her, but he was afraid of interrupting her breathing. So he settled for pressing his lips to her forehead instead.

She tasted bitter and smelled like a stale campfire. But she was here and alive and he was never going to let her go again.

"I love you, too," he said, holding her against his chest. "Never doubt it."

Chapter 14

Every time Isabel opened her eyes, she saw Wyatt.

He'd stayed with her while they'd waited for medical help to arrive, holding her close as they'd watched the barn burn. He'd jumped into the back of the ambulance with her, bouncing next to her as the EMTs had sped toward the hospital. He'd stood in the corner while the doctors examined her, his blue eyes alert and watchful as they'd checked her for injuries and treated her smoke inhalation.

And now he sat in the chair next to her hospital bed, resting for the first time in hours.

She studied his face for a moment, taking in the lines of fatigue around his eyes and mouth, the soot stains on his clothes and the skin of his arms. He'd been her rock during all of this, and she was never going to take him or their connection for granted again.

Just thinking about her earlier words made her blush with shame. How could she have been so shortsighted? Any other man would have taken her request for space and likely used it as an excuse to walk away. But Wyatt was here, supporting her and watching over her even though she'd pushed him away last night.

The fire had done more than destroy the barn. It had also stripped away her illusions of what was really important in life. She'd been so focused on trying to save the ranch, she'd very nearly thrown away her relationship with Wyatt. And for what? A need to feel like she was right?

She shook her head at the memory of their argument. Her fears about their compatibility had been overpowering at the time. But now that she'd literally been given a new lease on life, she recognized she'd given her worries too much control over her mind. Instead of thinking with a clear head, she'd been making decisions from a place of fear. And the worst part was she hadn't realized it. Probably wouldn't have, if not for her near-death experience.

Now, though, the haze was gone and she saw things as they truly were, not the way she'd misinterpreted them through her prism of stress and worry. Everyone she loved was alive. She and Diego were expected to make full recoveries. Even the cows and their calves were fine. In the end, wasn't that all that truly mattered?

Wyatt stirred and opened his eyes. When he caught her staring at him, he gave her one of those dazzling smiles that made her heart skip a beat.

"You're here."

He raised his arms above his head in a stretch that showed off his broad shoulders and toned stomach. "Told you I'd stay."

"How did I get so lucky?" she mused aloud.

"I'm glad you think it's luck," he replied. "Some women would find my constant presence annoying."

"They don't know what they're missing." It hurt to talk, but he was worth the pain. There were things she needed to say to him, things that couldn't wait.

"Are you sure about that?" His expression turned serious now, and he leaned forward. "Earlier, you said you wanted space. Now that I know you're going to be okay, I'm prepared to let you have it again."

Isabel shook her head before he finished speaking. The thought of him leaving triggered a wave of unhappiness that threatened to drown her newfound perspective on life. "No," she said, for emphasis. "Please don't go."

But what if he wanted to? What if he was still upset from their argument and he needed to do some thinking of his own? She wasn't going to force him to stay. If he needed his own time, she was going to have to be okay with that.

"Unless you want to leave," she amended. "I know I hurt you last night, and I'm sorry. If you need to re-think things where we're concerned, I'll understand."

"Hmm." The noncommittal sound made her anxiety spike as she anticipated the worst. "I'm more concerned about your feelings on the subject, to be honest with you."

She tilted her head to the side. "What do you mean?"

"I mean you seem to have had a complete change of heart since last night. I guess I want to make sure it's real and not a knee-jerk reaction you're having to almost dying." There was a hint of vulnerability in his gaze and Isabel realized he was worried she was going to jerk him around and hurt him again once the adrenaline of survival wore off.

"This isn't the trauma talking," she assured him. "Though I won't lie and say that has nothing to do with it." She shrugged. "I realized what's really important last night. And while the ranch is always going to be a part of my life, it shouldn't become my whole life. I see now that I was putting my worries about the future of the ranch before everything else. But I need to make sure *I* have a future, too, and I want you to be in it."

Wyatt nodded thoughtfully. "I'd like that," he said quietly.

She released her breath in a shuddering sigh that made her lungs ache. "I don't know why you put up with me," she said, smiling in relief. "But I'm so glad you do."

He got to his feet and leaned over the bed to kiss her softly. "We already lost ten years because of miscommunication," he said. "I don't want us to make that same mistake again."

"Me, neither." And yet they'd come close to doing just that, thanks to her earlier words.

"I know that look," Wyatt said, caressing her cheek with his fingertips. "Don't beat yourself up. We both made mistakes yesterday."

"I don't recall you trying to blow up our relationship," she joked.

"No, but I understand why you did," he said. "I haven't supported you like I should. I told you I'd help you brainstorm strategies for the ranch, but I didn't follow through. I knew you were already feeling isolated because Diego and your grandfather were pushing back against your suggestions. I should have tried to carry some of the load with you, but I didn't." He shook his head. "It's no wonder you wanted some space, when I was just another source of stress for you."

Isabel felt her jaw drop. The man was a mind reader; it was the only explanation for how he'd so perfectly articulated her thoughts.

He caught her expression and grinned. "I've had a lot of time to think," he replied. "And I minored in psychology."

"Amazing," she murmured.

"If you say so." He pulled the chair closer and sat, then reached for her hand. "I must say, though, I'm glad we talked about this. I would have left if you'd really wanted me to, but I wouldn't have gone far. Not now that someone's tried to kill you."

She pushed up in the bed, tired of laying back. "What happened exactly?" she asked. "I started out helping Diego and Peter with some difficult deliveries, and the next thing I know, the barn's on fire and the doors are stuck."

"Not just stuck," Wyatt said grimly. "Someone had wrapped a chain around them and locked it in place. There was no way you were getting out of there on your own."

"No wonder Peter didn't open the doors." The poor kid hadn't stood a chance. "I'm glad he ran for help."

"I don't think he did," Wyatt said. He leaned forward, his expression troubled. "I found him on the ground a few feet away from the doors. He was pretty out of it, clutching his head. He said you and Diego pushed him through the window, but when he came around to let you out, someone hit him on the head from behind."

"Oh my God." Horror filled her as she imagined the scene. "Is he all right?" He seemed like a nice kid and she'd been proud of the way he'd pushed through his fear to help her deliver the calf. He had the makings of a good cowboy and she hoped he would come through this nightmare intact.

"He'll be fine," Wyatt said. "The medics checked him out. He's got a nice knot on the back of his head, but that's all. You and Diego got him out before the smoke could hurt him."

She nodded, relieved at the news. But she couldn't enjoy the sensation. Something tugged at the edges of her mind, vying for attention.

"Did anyone notice a stranger last night? Someone running away?"

Wyatt shook his head. "Not that I know. The sheriff's deputies are at the ranch now, interviewing witnesses. I certainly didn't see anything like that, but then again, I wasn't looking, either."

The bottom of her world gave way and Isabel leaned back against the mattress, feeling suddenly light-headed.

"What's wrong?" Wyatt shot to his feet, alarmed at her sudden change.

She swallowed, squeezed his hand to show she was still okay. "If no one noticed a stranger last night, or saw anyone trying to run away, then that means…"

Understanding dawned in Wyatt's eyes. "Yeah," he confirmed, lowering himself back into the chair. "I was wondering how long it would take for you to piece it together."

"You already knew?"

He shrugged. "Like I said earlier, I've had a lot of time to think."

Tears filled her eyes and she blinked hard to dispel them. "I can't believe someone we know would do this." One by one, the faces of the people who worked at the ranch drifted through her mind. None of them seemed capable of locking her in a barn and setting it on fire, but that's exactly what had happened.

"I know it's a hard thing to come to grips with," Wyatt said softly. "Try not to think about it now. Focus on getting better, and let the sheriff and his men do their job."

Isabel knew he was right but her heart still ached. "How am I supposed to act now? I don't know who I can trust." Just the thought of returning to the house and having to be around the ranch hands was enough to make her palms sweat. How could she work with them knowing any one of them might have tried to kill her and Diego?

She'd come back to work on her family's ranch because she'd wanted a sense of connection, of belonging. But now she felt alone and vulnerable, surrounded by nameless, faceless hostile forces that threatened to destroy her and the land she loved so much.

"You can trust me." Wyatt's calm, deep voice broke through her mounting despair. She focused on the sound, grabbing onto it like a lifeline that she used to pull herself free of her emotional storm.

He was right, of course. She knew on a bone-deep level he'd never deliberately hurt her. Just as she knew her brother and Abuelo and Maria would always be there for her. Breath by breath, she began to rebuild her defenses until she no longer felt so exposed.

"I've never doubted that," she said.

"And you'll never have to." He leaned over and kissed her softly, gently. It was a simple kiss, hardly more than a whisper of his lips against hers. But there was such tenderness in the gesture, such love, that Isabel felt her heart completely melt.

"I love you," she said, reaching up to cup his cheek with her palm. She knew she'd already told him that, both when they were in the throes of their love-making and after he'd rescued her from the fire. But she wanted him to hear her say it when their emotions weren't running so high, so he would know she truly meant it. She never wanted to give him a reason to doubt the sincerity of her words again.

He smiled, his blue eyes practically glowing with emotion as he stared down at her. "I love you, too."

"Always have," she said.

"Always will," he finished.

"Finally!" Diego climbed out of the truck and turned his face to the sun. "I thought we were never going to get out of there."

"It was one night," Isabel grumbled. She took Wyatt's hand, allowing him to help her down. "But it is good to be home. It's hard to sleep in a hospital."

They both still sounded hoarse and Wyatt privately thought it wouldn't have been a bad thing to keep the siblings under watch for another day. But Isabel and Diego had been agitating to go home from the moment they'd been admitted, so it was no wonder the medical staff had finally relented.

They weren't the only ones who were happy to be home. Wyatt stretched, working out some of the kinks in his back and shoulders. The nurses had been kind enough to roll in a cot for his use last night and, while he'd slept, it hadn't been comfortable. He was looking forward to spending the night in a real bed, with Isabel tucked safely in his arms.

He glanced at the blackened remains of the barn, a shiver running through him at the visceral reminder of just how close he'd come to losing her. The smell of fire was still in the air. An acrid tang that would likely persist for a while, at least until they could get the mess cleaned up. The sheriff had told Jose to leave everything in place until they could establish exactly how the fire had been started. Apparently they were bringing in an arson investigator from El Paso to evaluate the wreckage and reconstruct the point of ignition. What might have been considered an unfortunate accident had been elevated to an attempted murder case, thanks to the chains that had held the doors shut.

"Damn." Diego shook his head as he stared at the site. "It's a total loss."

Isabel walked to her brother and placed her hand on his arm. "We'll rebuild."

He snorted. "At least we have insurance for the buildings." He glanced down at her. "I wish I could say the same for myself."

Wyatt's heart twisted in sympathy. His position as a park ranger provided medical benefits, but the same could not be said for self-employed ranchers. Diego had told him yesterday that he'd stopped buying health insurance for himself in a bid to cut costs.

Isabel's face crumpled in dismay. "Oh, Diego," she said. She snaked her arm around his waist in a supportive hug. "We'll figure it out."

He looked down at her, his expression apologetic. "Guess we should accept that offer, after all."

"No." Isabel shook her head. "We'll find another way." She slid a glance in Wyatt's direction and he nodded. They'd spent part of last night brainstorming strategies to deal with the ranch's financial difficulties, and they'd come up with the makings of what he thought was a solid plan.

"Let's go inside," Wyatt suggested. "I'm sure Jose is dying to see you both."

Isabel released her brother and slipped her hand in his as they started up the porch steps. It was a familiar gesture, the kind of thing he'd taken for granted before. But now that he'd been reminded of how fragile life really was, Wyatt knew he'd never overlook the simple connection again.

Diego entered the house first, triggering exclamations of happy surprise from Maria. She gave him a huge hug, grousing about his appearance and scolding him for scaring her so. Then she turned her attention to Isabel, who bore it all with a patient smile.

When she was done fussing over her wayward

chicks, she turned to Wyatt. He was surprised when she threw her arms around his waist and squeezed him tightly. "Thank you for bringing them back to me, *mijo*," she said. For a quick second, her façade slipped and he saw just how terrified she'd been.

Wyatt hugged her back. "They're fine, Tía. Everyone's okay."

Maria drew in a shaky breath and nodded. *"¡Gracias a Dios!"* She stepped back and crossed herself, then blinked, her mask in place once more. "Your *abuelo* is in his study. Go on."

Wyatt hung back as Diego and Isabel stepped forward. He didn't want to intrude on a personal family moment between the three of them. But Isabel turned and held out her hand.

"Come on," she said.

"Are you sure?"

She smiled, and his heart lightened. "Like it or not, you're part of this family."

He glanced at Diego, who nodded. "She's right. He's going to want to see you, too."

"All right, then." He followed them down the hall and filed into the small room behind them.

Jose looked up from his desk, his eyes filling with tears when he saw his grandchildren. *"Mis bebés,"* he murmured. He pushed out of his chair, arms extended. Isabel and Diego rushed forward and the three of them embraced, holding each other tightly. A lump formed in Wyatt's throat at the touching scene, and he felt honored to have been included in this moment.

"Never do that to me again," Jose scolded. "I already lost your father. I cannot lose my grandchildren, as well."

Diego chuckled. "Yes, sir."

"Sit, all of you. You must still be tired."

Wyatt settled onto the ancient love seat and draped his arm around Isabel when she sat next to him. A sense of peace stole over him as the family began to talk. There was something soothing about having everyone in this room, Isabel tucked against his side. It would be easy to pretend they were the only ones around, but he knew it was dangerous to indulge in that line of thought. Someone who worked for the ranch was behind the attacks, and if the barn fire was any indication, it was only a matter of time before one of the people in this room died.

"Did you speak to the sheriff?" Jose asked.

Both Diego and Isabel nodded. "One of the deputies came to my hospital room," she said.

"Same for me," Diego added.

Jose nodded. "Then you know they suspect one of our employees." He sounded tired, and Wyatt felt sorry for the older man. Not only was he dealing with the stress of almost losing his family, he was having to process the realization that one of the people they trusted was behind the attacks. It was a bitter pill to swallow and he knew Isabel and Diego were struggling with it, as well.

"I think we can safely rule out Peter," Isabel said. "He was with us at the time, and whoever chained the doors shut attacked him, too."

"That only leaves ten other people," Diego said with a frown. "Not exactly a short list."

"And not your job, either," Wyatt reminded them. "I know you want to figure out who's behind this, but the sheriff's department is working on it. They're not going to forget about a case of arson and attempted murder."

Diego opened his mouth to protest but Isabel cut him off.

"He's right," she said. "We can talk about this until we're blue in the face, but it's not going to solve anything. Besides—" she glanced at Wyatt "—there's something else I want to discuss with you both."

"What's that?" Jose asked.

She took a deep breath and Wyatt gave her a reassuring squeeze.

"I've been thinking about our financial situation," Isabel said. "And Wyatt and I may have come up with a solution. We've been so focused on keeping things the way they are, but what if we tried something completely different? We could become a dude ranch for special-needs children."

"A dude ranch?" Jose sounded the words out as if they were foreign. "What does that mean?"

"It means we bring families in to experience life on a working ranch." She leaned forward, her excitement building as she spoke. "A lot of people are curious as to what life is like as a cowboy. And based on the research Wyatt and I have done, children with special needs can really benefit from contact with animals. Plus, it would be a nice break for their families—a vacation from the stresses of their daily lives. We could offer them an authentic experience—horseback riding, checking fences, helping herd the animals. Even branding, after calving season ends. And we could have things like cookouts and hayrides, maybe even a petting zoo."

Diego's expression was unreadable but Wyatt could tell he was listening.

Isabel forged ahead. "We could offer different packages. We'd start out small—just daytime tours and activities. Then, as the business grew, we could build some small cabins and designate some pastures as campsites so families could stay overnight if they wanted. We could even offer retreats in conjunction with the children's hospital in Alpine."

"And how are we going to pay for all this?" Diego asked softly. "We'd need extra horses for the families, extra hands to help with the people. And do you expect Maria to do all of the cooking for these guests? Not to mention, how are we going to pay for the food?"

She met her brother's gaze. "We'll have to sell off part of the herd. It would represent a real shift in our focus. Basically, we'd have to pivot from being a cattle ranch to a nonprofit organization. We'd keep a small group of animals, of course. But instead of relying on the cattle trade for our living, we'd focus on bringing an authentic experience to the families who come here."

"You really think there's a market for this?" Diego shook his head. "Hardly anyone comes out here."

"I'm not saying it will be easy," Isabel replied. "But I think if we play up the history of our land and our ranch, the people will come. We can offer deals to the families coming to Big Bend." She glanced at Wyatt. He nodded, pride welling in his chest as he watched her describe her vision. "We're so close, we could advertise it as a day trip for park visitors with special-needs children."

"It would be a huge change." Diego leaned back in his chair and folded his hands in front of his chest.

"But perhaps a good one?" Jose remarked.

"Sounds like a lot of investment up front," her brother said. "Which brings us back to our current situation. We don't have piles of money lying around."

"I'm not saying we have to go all-in immediately," she said. "We could transition over time, keep the costs low until things start to really get going. And since we'd be functioning as a nonprofit, we'd be eligible to apply for grant funding from different organizations."

Wyatt reached for her hand, gave it a gentle squeeze. "It's an excellent idea," he said quietly. "And I'm not just saying that because I'm biased."

She smiled at him, clearly grateful for his support.

"What made you change your mind?" Diego asked. "Before the fire, you still thought we should sell the mineral rights and be done with it. Why don't you want us to do that anymore?"

Isabel lifted her chin and Wyatt saw a glint of anger in her eyes. "Someone came onto our land and tried to destroy our livelihood. They undermined our business and sought to break us. I realized the energy company would be the same, in a way. If we sold them the mineral rights, our land would no longer truly be our own. I'm not willing to voluntarily hand over control like that. Not after coming so close to losing it at the hands of a traitor."

A slow smile spread over Diego's face. "I should have known your type-A tendencies would win in the end."

Isabel gave her brother an indignant look that made Wyatt laugh. When she turned it on him, he held up his hands. "Face it," he told her. "Your brother is right. You do like to be in charge."

"There's nothing wrong with that," she grumbled.

"I didn't say there was," he agreed.

"Never apologize for your strength, *mija*," Jose instructed with a paternal smile.

Maria appeared in the doorway. "Are you all hungry?" she asked hopefully.

"Starving." Diego stood and grinned at her. "Are you offering to feed me?"

"Only at the table," she replied. "Like civilized people."

"A small price to pay," Diego said. He moved to his grandfather's side, ready to help the older man from his chair. But Jose waved away the silent offer of assistance.

"I'm not that old," he said, pushing to his feet.

Wyatt smiled as he watched the two of them leave the study. Then he glanced down at Isabel, happy to see her smiling, as well.

"It's strange," she mused as they started to follow the lunch crowd. "Even though we still don't know who's trying to hurt us, I feel hopeful about our future." She glanced up at him. "Am I just in denial?"

"Nope." Wyatt took her hand as they walked. "I think it's better to focus on the positive. There will be plenty of time later to start worrying again."

She laughed. "I never thought I'd procrastinate when it comes to stress."

Her description made him smile. "It's always good to try something new."

Isabel settled next to Wyatt on the sofa and opened her laptop. Diego sat in one of the large armchairs, and both Abuelo and Maria were sitting in the sofa nearest the fireplace. They'd all come here to talk more about her proposal to turn the Cruz ranch into a nonprofit organization.

Lunch had been a short affair, as both she and Diego had needed to check on the animals. She'd been pleased to discover the three cattle and their calves all looking well, with the babies nursing as their mothers grazed. None of the animals seemed injured by their experience in the fire, which was another reminder of just how lucky they'd been.

Diego had checked in with the ranch hands who were monitoring the herd in the fields. The reports had all been good, so they'd headed back to the house to continue planning the future of the ranch.

Isabel knew she shouldn't be looking for trouble, but she couldn't help but feel like the worst was yet to come.

Wyatt rubbed her shoulders. "It's okay," he murmured.

"How do you always seem to know what I'm thinking?" It wasn't the first time he'd accurately picked up on her mood. It was a habit she found simultaneously endearing and annoying. It was nice feeling so connected to him, but couldn't she have a few secrets?

He chuckled, the low sound wrapping around her like a warm blanket. "You have a glass face," he said quietly.

"I didn't think I was *that* bad."

"You're not," he assured her. "But I pay attention." He winked and a shiver of anticipation shot down her spine.

"All right," Diego said loudly, interrupting their private moment. "Let's talk about how we can make this work."

Over the next hour, they discussed options, made plans and drew up a list of questions that required the input of an attorney. Isabel loved every minute of it. For the first time in what seemed like forever, they were all working toward a common goal instead of arguing with each other over competing visions of the future.

The doorbell chimed, interrupting their discussion.

Diego tilted his head to the side and shot a questioning look at Abuelo.

"I'm not sure," her grandfather said. "The sheriff, perhaps?"

"I'll go," Wyatt volunteered.

He returned a moment later with their visitor.

"Gabriel," Abuelo said. He rose and gestured for the other man to join them, then sat back down. "This is a surprise."

Gabriel nodded and looked at everyone uncertainly. "I'm sorry I didn't warn you I was coming. I probably should have called first."

"Have a seat." Abuelo indicated the recliner next to Diego.

Gabriel lowered himself into the chair, but Isabel could tell by the tension in his body he wasn't comfortable.

"What's going on?" she asked, trying to break the ice.

He met her gaze, a flash of gratitude in his eyes.

"I heard about what happened here. Is everyone okay?"

"We are," Diego replied. "We got lucky."

"I saw the ruins on the way in." Gabriel shook his head. "I'm glad the fire didn't spread."

"So are we," Abuelo said with a thin smile.

"Will you rebuild?" he asked.

Diego and Isabel exchanged a look. How much of their plan should they reveal right now? If Gabriel really was a Cruz, he was entitled to a say. But he was still too much of an unknown for Isabel to feel comfortable bringing him fully into the loop. Until she knew she could trust him, she preferred to keep things close to the vest.

"We hope to," she said, keeping her answer deliberately vague.

He nodded, but his distracted expression made her wonder if he'd really heard what she'd said.

"I, uh. I have the results of the DNA test." He stood and pulled an envelope from the back pocket of his pants and tapped it against his palm. "I thought maybe we should open it together." He walked over to Abuelo and extended his arm. "Would you like to do the honors?"

Isabel's breath caught in her throat as her grandfather reached up to take the envelope. Wyatt placed his hand on her shoulder, but she couldn't look away as Abuelo slid his finger under the flap and broke the seal.

He withdrew a folded piece of paper and studied

it. A frown spread across his face and she could tell he was trying to make sense of the information on the page.

"But this says…" He looked up with a confused expression.

Gabriel reached for the paper.

Abuelo passed it to him and then met Isabel's gaze. He shook his head slightly, as though he couldn't believe what he'd just read.

A sense of trepidation filled her. Something unexpected was happening here. But, based on her grandfather's reaction, she couldn't tell if it was a positive or negative development.

"But this doesn't make sense." Gabriel looked up, his expression a mix of frustration and pleading. "It says our Y chromosomes don't match. That means…" His voice faded as he shook his head.

"It means you're not a Cruz," Diego finished quietly. Isabel glanced at her brother, expecting to find a gleam of triumph in his eyes. But she saw only pity as he watched Gabriel.

"I don't understand," Gabriel said. His voice was tight with distress, his muscles tense. "Mom left me a letter telling me about her affair with Ricardo. The check was inside. She told me to bring the check to you, and it would prove my identity."

"I'm so sorry," Abuelo said softly. "I thought you were my grandson."

"But…" Gabriel frowned, clearly confused. "If Ricardo Cruz is not my father, then who is?"

"That would be me, I expect."

Everyone turned at the sound of the new voice. A shock zinged through Isabel as she recognized Ruben standing in the doorway.

What on earth?

Just as the question formed in her mind, Ruben stepped into the room. But Isabel recognized in an instant he wasn't the same calm, dependable man she'd always known.

This was a side of Ruben she'd never seen before. He was a stranger.

And he was carrying a gun.

Chapter 15

Wyatt caught sight of the gun and moved without thinking. He was too far away to try to disarm Ruben, but he could do his best to protect Isabel.

He positioned himself in front of her, blocking her from Ruben's view. The other man flicked a glance in his direction, but otherwise didn't acknowledge him.

Ruben advanced into the room, his eyes darting from Gabriel to Jose. "Your mother was my girl-friend," he said. He kept his arm down, gun pointed at the floor. But Wyatt felt the agitation coming off of him in waves and knew it was only a matter of time before he did something rash.

"What?" Gabriel appeared even more confused.

He looked from Jose to Ruben, seeking clarification. "Who are you?"

"What's the meaning of this, Ruben?" Jose pushed to his feet and stepped to the side, drawing Ruben's attention away from Maria. She shrank back into the corner of the sofa, terror etched on her face.

"Don't pretend you don't know." Ruben didn't raise his voice, but venom dripped from every word he spoke. "Christine was a good girl. We loved each other. Your son—" he turned and spat onto the wood floor "—seduced her. He poured lies into her ear, promising to leave his wife and marry her, to make her the queen of the Cruz ranching empire. She believed him." He shook his head in disgust.

"Then she realized she was pregnant. I begged her to come back to me. Told her I'd raise the baby with her no matter who its father was. But she refused. Said Ricardo was going to take care of her." He laughed, but there was no humor in it. "As if Ricardo had ever taken care of anyone in his life."

Wyatt saw Diego open his mouth. He shook his head, warning his friend to keep his thoughts to himself. Now was not the time to defend his father's honor.

If Ruben had noticed their silent communication, he didn't acknowledge it. "Ricardo broke her heart," he continued. "Once again, I pleaded with her to let me help. I was too late, though. She said she'd already made up her mind. That she couldn't stay here because she didn't want to spend the rest of her life reminded of her broken heart. So she came to you."

"Yes," Jose confirmed, swallowing hard. "She asked me for money. I gave it to her. It seemed like the right thing to do at the time."

With Ruben's attention focused on Jose, Wyatt made a small gesture to try to get Isabel to stand. If he could get her on her feet, he could distract Ruben so she and Maria would have a chance to escape.

He couldn't risk turning around to look at her, but after a few seconds, he felt her fingers brush his own and then her hand lightly touched the center of his back.

Relief washed over him, but he wasn't about to celebrate just yet.

"She left after you gave her the check," Ruben continued. "I was devastated."

"Why did you stay?" Diego spoke for the first time, voicing the question they were all thinking. "Why not quit, get away from this place?"

Ruben's smile was full of malice. "Revenge. I wanted to hurt your father, but after he died, I had to reconsider."

"Ricardo has been dead for years," Jose said. "Why act now?"

Ruben looked at Gabriel, a flash of longing showing on his face. "I got a letter about three months ago from your mother. She told me she'd changed her mind and kept the baby. She also told me she still didn't know if you were mine, but that she was going to make sure you came back here so we could find out."

Gabriel went pale as the words sank in, and Wyatt

felt bad for the guy. Not only had he lost his mother a few months ago, now he was discovering she was a liar who had played on his desire for a family in the worst way.

"You set the traps."

Wyatt tensed as Isabel spoke from behind him. *What are you doing?* He wanted to shake her for drawing attention to herself rather than sneaking out of the room.

Ruben turned, moved until he could see her. "I did."

"Why?" Diego asked. He looked genuinely baffled.

"The offer," Isabel said before Ruben could reply.

Wyatt heard a dawning understanding in her voice and knew she had put the pieces together.

"That's right." Ruben nodded in her direction. "You always were the smart one."

"You were trying to run us into the ground, to force us to sell the rights."

"That doesn't make sense." Diego's confusion mirrored his own, but Wyatt was more interested in getting Isabel to safety than in solving this particular mystery.

He took a step to block Isabel from view once more, but Ruben saw him and shook his head. "You stay there." He raised his arm, aiming the gun at Wyatt's chest.

Wyatt froze, wanting to make sure he didn't give Ruben an excuse to shoot.

"Why did you want us to take the deal?" Jose said, drawing Ruben's attention away from Wyatt once more. "The money would have saved the ranch. You can't possibly want that."

"I'm playing the long game, friend," Ruben said. "Can you imagine how much damage a fracking well accident causes? I've done some research, and let me tell you, it's not pretty."

"You're crazy." Isabel whispered the words but Ruben heard her nonetheless.

He turned to look at her. "No, not crazy," he said. "Just patient."

"Not patient enough," Isabel said. "You set the barn on fire, didn't you?"

Her question triggered a snippet of memory; the orange glow of the flames reflecting in Ruben's belt buckle. Wyatt hadn't thought anything of it at the time, but now he recognized that Ruben had been fully clothed, while everyone else there had been in various stages of undress thanks to the late hour.

Ruben shrugged. "You weren't making a decision quickly enough."

"And now?" Jose asked. "What's your next move?"

"I'm not sure," Ruben replied. "Your family has taken so much from me. At first, I thought perhaps I should just kill you and be done with it. But that wouldn't really cause you pain, would it, Jose?"

Fear flickered across the old man's face and Wyatt's stomach twisted as he heard what Ruben hadn't yet said.

"You took my child from me," Ruben said. "I think I'll return the favor."

Time seemed to slow as Ruben began to turn toward Isabel. Acting on instinct, Wyatt twisted and grabbed the laptop from its spot on the cushion. He hurled it like an oversize Frisbee at Ruben.

The computer struck Ruben's leg with a satisfying thump and he let out a startled cry. Wyatt charged, tackling Ruben just as he fired. The gun went off with an explosive bang and a split second later, they landed with a bone-jarring impact. The next thing he knew, Diego was there, kneeling next to him and holding Ruben's arm down.

"Isabel!" He yelled her name, unwilling to take his eyes off Ruben until he was sure the man no longer posed a threat. "Talk to me!"

When she didn't respond right away, he began to panic. He pushed off the floor and whirled around, only to collide with her. "Why didn't you answer me?" He held her at arm's length and ran his gaze over her body, searching for signs of injury.

She tapped him urgently on the arm. He looked up and frowned when he saw her lips were moving. She *was* trying to talk to him—he just couldn't hear her.

Wyatt shook his head and pointed to his ear. She nodded and reached out to wipe her fingers along the side of his neck. When she held them up, he saw a smear of bright red blood on her fingertips.

He sank onto the sofa, gingerly touching the shell

of his ear. The gunshot must have ruptured his eardrum. And now that his adrenaline was starting to fade, the pain was becoming more noticeable.

"Is everyone okay?" He could tell by the look on Isabel's face that he was yelling, but he needed to make sure no one else had been hurt. She nodded and gave him a thumbs-up.

Maria came over and took his hand, pulling him up from the sofa. She gestured for him to follow her, clearly wanting to lead him out of the room. Wyatt resisted—he didn't want to leave Isabel.

Maria said something and Isabel nodded. She touched his arm, urging him forward.

Before he left, he turned to look at Diego, trying to gauge if his friend needed his help. He might not be able to hear, but his arms and legs still worked and he could lend a hand to keep Ruben under control until the sheriff arrived.

Diego shook his head and waved him away. *Thank you*, he mouthed from across the room.

Wyatt gave his friend a small salute then turned around. His head was pounding, his knees ached from the impact with the floor, and he'd somehow managed to bite his tongue during the scuffle. But the pain receded to insignificance when he caught sight of Isabel waiting for him.

The woman he loved held out her hand with a small smile. Wyatt moved to join her and, together, they took a step into their future.

Two weeks later...

They sat in the living room again. Isabel would have preferred to talk elsewhere, but Abuelo had insisted they reclaim the space.

"We cannot let one bad incident ruin all the good memories we've made there," he'd said firmly.

He was right and Isabel recognized that the sooner they stopped treating the room like a haunted space, the faster the lingering psychic effects of Ruben's attack would disappear.

Still, she'd felt a shiver of unease as she'd walked into the room. Would she ever be able to sit in here without the memories of Ruben's hateful words and violent act running through her mind?

Recognizing her discomfort, Wyatt placed his arm around her shoulder and drew her in close. She leaned into his embrace, drawing comfort from his touch.

"Thanks for letting me in." Gabriel glanced around the room, his manner subdued.

"Of course." Abuelo nodded. "You are welcome here anytime."

"I, uh, I wanted to apologize. Again," he added, his cheeks flushing pink.

"It's all good," Diego said. "Like we told you before, we don't hold you responsible for Ruben's actions."

Gabriel acknowledged this with a quick smile. "I appreciate that. But I still feel like I made things worse. If I hadn't made such a stink about being a

Cruz..." He looked down. "Well, there's no way to know what might have been."

Isabel's heart went out to the man. It was clear he wanted to belong to a family, to have the kind of bonds that stood the test of time. They'd gotten off to a rocky start, but maybe, over time, he could become a Cruz in spirit, if not in name.

"Are you going to start rebuilding the barn soon?"

It was an obvious change of subject, but Isabel understood he wanted to move on.

"Yes," she said. They'd spoken earlier about the plans to turn the ranch into a nonprofit organization offering services for special-needs children. Gabriel had been impressed by their plans, making her even more excited about the project. "We've started clearing the rubble, but it's probably going to take a while. The insurance company will only pay what they estimate the structure was worth, and it's going to cost more than that to build a new barn."

Gabriel nodded. "That's kind of why I'm here. I think I can help with that." He punched something into his phone then flipped the screen around and passed it to Isabel.

She stared at the screen, trying to make sense of what she was seeing.

It looked like a fund-raising website. The words **SUPPORT CRUZ RANCH** ran along the top in big, bold type.

"What is this?" Confusion mounted as she scrolled down the page. There was a brief description of the barn fire, along with links to what looked like several news articles. There was also an outline of their plan to become a dude ranch for special-needs children.

Wyatt leaned over, while Diego and Abuelo moved to stand behind her, reading over her shoulder. Someone had set up a collection page, asking for donations from the public to help rebuild the barn and raise start-up funds for the nonprofit. That was unexpected enough, but when she saw the amount of money that had already been raised, she couldn't believe her eyes.

She looked up at Gabriel, searching for an explanation.

He shrugged, smiling shyly. "I wanted to help. I'm not good at ranching, but I do know my way around a computer."

"But all this money…" She gestured to the website. "Where is it coming from?"

"The fire made the news," he explained. "And not just in the nearby towns. Networks across the state have run stories about it, and the fact that it was no ordinary blaze. Everyone is glad you all survived, and they want to help you rebuild and recover. I set up this website so they could contribute."

"I don't know what to say." She shook her head then glanced at Diego and Abuelo.

Abuelo's eyes were shiny with unshed tears. "Young man," he said, drawing Gabriel in for a hug. "Thank you. Thank you so much."

Even Diego seemed touched. He grabbed Gabriel's hand and pumped hard, his Adam's apple bobbing as he tried to speak.

"You don't have to say anything," Gabriel replied. "I needed to make amends. I know you don't think I have anything to be sorry for, but I had to do this for my own peace of mind."

Isabel turned to look at Wyatt. He appeared as shocked as the rest of them.

She opened her mouth but Gabriel held up his hand. "Don't try to tell me you can't accept the money," he said, successfully anticipating her objection. "The people who have donated did so because they wanted to help. You need to respect their wishes, if nothing else."

"Hard to argue with that," Diego muttered.

Isabel turned back to the screen, her mind whirling as she tried to process the surprise. With this amount of money, they could rebuild the barn and start the transformation from working cattle ranch into a dude ranch for special-needs children and their families. They could start to partner with specialists, begin training the horses for equine therapy…the list was long, but now they had the funds to tackle it in earnest.

It was really happening. They were going to take the leap.

She passed the phone back to Gabriel and leaned against Wyatt once more. His strength did more than prop her up—his presence and his unwavering support over the past few weeks had given her the courage to take the lead as they had committed to this new venture.

"This calls for tequila!" Abuelo announced. "Come,

let us go to my study. That's where I keep the good stuff."

"You say you're good at websites?" Diego clapped Gabriel on the back as they headed for the door. "I have a proposal for you…" His voice faded as they moved down the hall toward Abuelo's study.

Once they were alone, Wyatt pressed a kiss to the top of her head. "You okay?"

He was still recovering from a perforated eardrum, so she nodded to make it easier on him.

She pulled away to let him see her face when she spoke. "I just can't believe this is happening."

His eyes sparkled with excitement. "It's like a sign, don't you think?"

"I do, now that you mention it." Isabel normally didn't put much stock in the idea of fate or karma, but the timing of this windfall was too perfect to be denied.

"I'm so proud of you," Wyatt said.

His words sent a tingle racing through her limbs. Wyatt's opinion meant a lot to her, more even than that of Abuelo's.

"Thank you," she said, cupping his cheek with her palm.

"For what?"

"Believing in me. Supporting me. Not giving up on me."

Wyatt laughed. "You make it sound like I'm some kind of saint."

"You mean you're not?" she teased.

"Hardly." He reached for her, pulling her close so he could fit his mouth over hers.

Isabel sank into the kiss, reveling in the tickling rasp of his stubble against her skin, the warm heat of his mouth and the faint minty flavor of his toothpaste. It was a combination that made her knees weak and, she suspected, always would.

He pulled away after a moment, his eyes shining with tenderness as he looked at her face. "Ready for that tequila?" he asked. "We've got a lot to celebrate."

"Only if you're coming with me," she said.

"Of course I am." He got to his feet, held out his hand to help her stand. "Haven't you realized you're stuck with me now?"

She slid her palm against his, her heart light and her spirits high. "Lucky me."

* * * * *

*Don't miss the previous books in Lara Lacombe's
Rangers of Big Bend series,
available now from
Harlequin Romantic Suspense!*

Ranger's Baby Rescue
Ranger's Justice

Get 4 FREE REWARDS!

We'll send you 2 FREE Books plus 2 FREE Mystery Gifts.

Harlequin Romantic Suspense books are heart-racing page-turners with unexpected plot twists and irresistible chemistry that will keep you guessing to the very end.

FREE
Value Over
$20

*The town of Baywood is on edge after a series of bizarre
murders. Detectives A.L. McKittridge and Rena Morgan
will stop at nothing to catch this elusive killer before he
strikes again...*

Keep reading for a sneak peek at
Ten Days Gone *by Beverly Long.*

A.L. rode shotgun while Rena drove. He liked to look
around, study the landscape. Jane Picus had lived
within the city limits of Baywood. The fifty-thousand-
person city bordered the third-largest lake in west-
central Wisconsin, almost halfway between Madison
and Eau Claire. While the town was generally peaceful,
that many people in a square radius of thirteen miles
could do some damage to one another. Add in the
weekend boaters, who were regularly overserved, and
the Baywood Police Department dealt with the usual
assortment of crime. Burglary. Battery. Drugs. The
occasional arson.

And murder. There had been two the previous year.
One was a family dispute, and the killer had been quickly
apprehended. The other was a workplace shooter who'd
turned the gun on himself after killing his boss. Neither
had been pleasant, but they hadn't shaken people's
belief that Baywood was a good place to live and raise a
family. People were happy when their biggest complaint
was about the size of the mosquitoes.

Now, for-sale signs were popping up in yards. There would likely be more by next week. Four unsolved murders in forty days was bad. Bad for tourism, bad for police morale and certainly bad for the poor women and their families.

In less than ten minutes, they were downtown. Brick sidewalks bordered both sides of Main Street for a full six blocks. Window boxes, courtesy of the garden club, were overflowing with petunias. The police department had moved to its new building in the three-hundreds block over ten years ago. Even then, it hadn't been new, but the good citizens of Baywood had voted to put some money into the sixty-year-old former department store. There was too much glass for A.L.'s comfort on the first floor and too little air-conditioning on the second and third. But it beat the hell out of working in the factory at the edge of town.

Which was where his father and his uncle Joe still worked. The McKittridge brothers. They'd been born and raised in Baywood, raised their own families there and had never left.

A.L. had sworn that wouldn't be his life. Yet here he was.

Because of Traci. His sixteen-year-old daughter.

Don't miss Ten Days Gone *by Beverly Long,*
available February 18, 2020 wherever
MIRA books and ebooks are sold.

MIRABooks.com

MEXPBL958